# Demonic
# DORA

## BEWITCHED IN HELL

AN AWARD-WINNING NOVEL IN
### THE DEMON DIARIES

# CLAIRE CHILTON

First published in Great Britain by Ragz Books 2013

This edition published by Ragz Books 2017

Copyright © 2012 by Claire Chilton

Published in Great Britain by Ragz Books

ISBN-10: 1908822635
ISBN-13: 978-1908822635

## Bibliography

Pratchett, Terry. (2012).
A Blink of the Screen: Collected Shorter Fiction.
Great Britain, Double Day.

# MORE BOOKS

## THE DEMON DIARIES
A Hint of Magic
Bewitched by Magic

Demonic Dora
Bewitched in Hell

Deceased Dora
Bewitched in Death

Divine Dora
Bewitched in Heaven

A Hint of Hell
Bewitched by Christmas

# DEDICATIONS

This book is dedicated to Jonathan Eldred for his wicked wit and creative additions to every chapter.

# ACKNOWLEDGEMENTS

I'd like to thank my mother for never being like Lady Lascher, for which I am eternally grateful.

Thanks to Kevin Weinberg, Eileen Gormley and Derek Landy for their wonderful advice and listening to my constant, unending, random and bizarre questions about this book.

I'd also like to thank all the wonderful fans and beta readers from Wattpad for joining me on this journey. I hope you laughed as often as I did.

"Mankind isn't really evil. It hasn't got enough
dignity to be evil."
- *A Blink of the Screen: Collected Shorter Fiction*
*Terry Pratchett (2012) p50.*

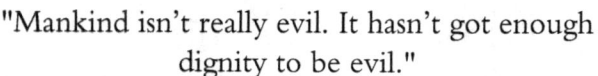

D ora Carridine rested her Doc Martens on the
wooden church pew in front of her and idly
cleaned her nails with a combat knife. She
watched the small film crew set up around the podium at
the front of the church while her father, the Reverend
Theodore Carridine, had his hair fluffed into angelic
white fuzz by a stylist.

She yawned. *Another bible bashing show coming
soon to a TV near you!* She didn't ask for much in life,
but she'd greatly appreciate it if the studio would cancel
her father's embarrassing television show. She didn't pray
to deities. Surely if there were such things as Gods, they'd
have listened when she begged them to burn her mother
alive for making her wear a cardigan in the eighth grade.

Dora had been a curious child, so when growing up
in such a strict religious home, she'd tested out as many
sins as she could. Lightning had never struck her down,
she hadn't incurred the wrath of God and to be honest, if

there was anyone up there watching, they didn't give a crap what she did.

"Now let us pray," her father said into the microphone when he stood at the podium, his face solemn.

Dora lowered her head and read the spell book in her lap. Images of demons and the blackest of magic filled the grimoire. She could barely read it. *I so wish I'd taken Latin now.*

"Our father, who art ..." Her father recited. The large congregation chanted with him.

"... Who art embarrassing whenst he is on television," Dora mumbled out of habit. Two devout parishioners spun around and glowered at her. "Hollowed be thy brain," she added for their benefit and chuckled when they turned away from her in disgust.

It was going to be a long show today, and she was already bored—beyond death. She glanced around the large church. People around her were praying with their eyes closed. Even her producer mother had her eyes shut and wasn't watching the show. *Time to get outta here.*

Dora shoved her spell book down the waistband of her red miniskirt and carefully lowered her feet off the pew. She slid the knife into the scabbard inside her boot before silently sinking down in her seat. She slipped onto the hard stone floor, rolling on all fours before she crawled through the narrow space between the pews. She sped up when she left the benches behind and was out in the open, scurrying towards the confessional boxes.

She rested behind the dark mahogany box before peering back at the room. No one was watching her.

They were all standing and preparing to sing a hymn. She stood up and walked into the alcove ahead, then climbed the stone staircase towards her room.

She brushed the dust off the knees of her red and black striped pantyhose on her way up. *Lazy ass cleaners should be crucified for the mess they left the place in.*

When she reached the top of the stairs, she turned left at the large organ pipes, heading up the narrow stone passage of a second staircase, which led to her attic room.

Dora's room was pretty cool. It was inside the spire of the old church, offering her privacy from the rest of the world. She pushed open the ancient oak door. It made a loud, ominous creak—just how she liked it. The room was not decorated to her liking with baby pink walls and a matching carpet. The little princess room was her parents' doing. She couldn't count the number of times she'd spray painted blood-red pentagrams or black demon art on the walls of this room. Every time she came back from school, it was back to princess pink with decorative voile hanging over the bed and pink fluffy throw cushions on the furniture.

Bile rose in her throat when she glanced down at the pink floral-print duvet. She swallowed and knelt on the floor at the end of her bed before pulling out the large white plastic sheet from beneath it. The sheet was actually the back of a Twister mat, but it worked just as well for a dark arts summoning circle. She had painted a black and red pentagram on it to put it to a darker use than it was intended for, meaning she had to ensure it was well hidden from her parents at all times.

3

She shivered with excitement. Today was going to be her day. After years of trying and failing, she was finally going to cast a spell that would work. Despite years of failure, her inability to summon a demon hadn't dimmed her enthusiasm. The Wicca group at the local magical supply store would be laughing at her on the other side of their white-light Earth-mother faces if she pulled this off.

Dora was going to summon a demon, and not just a normal demon. No, she was going for a high-level demon that would be under her control. *The first thing he's going to do for me is make this room red.*

She placed six black candles around her makeshift summoning circle and lit them one by one. She put an ornate pottery bowl at the center of the circle and threw a mixture of herbs into it. Next, she pulled the knife out of her boot and made a small cut on her thumb with it. She watched her blood slowly drip into the bowl until there were six drops. Then she pressed her thumb against her leg. Once the cut had stopped bleeding, she dropped the knife and dragged her schoolbag over to her. She reached inside it, feeling for the small box in the bottom of the bag.

The secret ingredient was a Karabashi bloodstone. She carefully opened the small black box and stared at the red shiny stone in awe. It looked like a glass ball filled with blood. She'd searched high and low for one when she'd found the spell in her book. None of the usual haunts had one; not the antiques shop or even the specialist magic supply store. She had tried everywhere and had nearly given up altogether. One stormy night when she'd been staring at the dark skies, she'd had a moment of clarity. After some tough negotiation, she'd got it on Ebay.

Dora put the bloodstone in the bowl and picked up the grimoire. Her heart thundered in her chest. It was going to work, it was. She could feel it. She carefully read the spell and closed her eyes, chanting with a faith she'd never felt before. Six times, she repeated the spell, and she waited.

She held her breath. A demon was going to appear—he was! Her clock ticked loudly as she sat cross-legged in front of her summoning circle, waiting. After a few silent moments, she let out her breath in an exhausted sigh. *Nothing again. Nothing ever works!*

She abruptly stood up and kicked over the bowl, shattering the bloodstone inside it. The thick, gloopy liquid slithered across the broken glass and mingled inside the bowl. She didn't bother to glance at it. She stormed out of her room and slammed the door shut behind her. *Nothing ever bloody works!*

Once Dora had left the room, a fire ignited in the center of the circle, and the Twister mat curled up as it became inflamed in the fires of hell.

# HELL ON EARTH

Josie Carridine watched from the front row pew as sweat dripped down her husband's face while he shouted at the TV cameras from the pulpit, threatening the wrath of God to all sinners. She nodded in agreement when he declared all vegetarians were an abomination. She was surely blessed to have such a righteous man for a husband. Not only had he saved her from a life of sin, pole dancing at the infamous 'Big Fat Joint', he'd also helped her career as a TV producer. Oh yes, life was wonderful once you left sin behind.

"And He shall strike you down," Theodore shouted out to his congregation. "Down to the depths of hell if— I-if ..."

Theodore stopped speaking and stared at the back of the church with his mouth hanging open and his eyes widening. Josie jumped when she heard a loud scream from the back of the room. She spun around to look behind her while hearing the entire congregation shifting in their seats as they did the same.

Thick black swirls of smoke were twirling in the air around the closed doors of the church. *Has someone set the doors on fire?* She gaped at the fog in shock and shook her head at the thought. The mist wasn't behaving like smoke at all. It amassed into a big black blob with more and more seeping in under the door until it split into two foggy shadows.

She lifted her glasses, which were hanging around her neck, to peer through them. The two black smoky shapes formed into separate entities that appeared to have heads and arms. She dropped her glasses and rubbed her eyes before looking again.

At the same time, both shadows snapped open fiery red eyes. Their maws gaped as they let out a loud hollow laugh that echoed through the church. Josie winced when Mrs. Smiggins, the oldest member of the congregation, keeled over three aisles down. *I hope she's fainted, and she's not dead.*

The two shadows each gripped a handle of the double doors of the church and flung them open. A burst of flames shot through the entrance. Gale force winds blasted through the room, knocking parishioners over and sending the smaller ones flying around the church in a twister style hurricane.

Josie ducked down in her seat and hugged the pew, which was thankfully nailed down.

"Out, damned demon." She heard Theodore shout at the shadows, but they had already evaporated into the flames. Lightning shot around the high ceiling of the church, shattering through the stained-glass windows. The air was alive with electricity.

Josie fell to her knees and prayed—and this time she meant it. *Dear God, please save me from this nightmare. I promise to be faithful and end my affair with Phil on camera four. I'll remain good and pious, and stop trying to sell ad space on the church website. Amen.*

She glanced up to see an army of turquoise serpents slithering through the doors and up the aisles towards the congregation, who were now screaming and running towards the pulpit to escape the demon snakes. She pulled herself up and jumped back as one of the snakes snapped at her hand, almost succeeding in ripping one of her fingers off. She pulled away just in time. They were like no snakes she'd ever seen before. Their eyes were ocean-blue, and their teeth were green. *Have they been drinking NiQuil?*

The snake reared up. It was as tall as she was. Fear slammed through her, making her knees tremble. It launched at her, emitting a deadly hiss. She threw her bible at it, knocking it backwards before she dashed towards the podium and cowered behind her husband, who continued to pray, although his voice was now hoarse.

The wind howled around them. The parishioners who hadn't passed out were all cowering around the pulpit. Some were white with shock, others were openly crying with thick trails of snot pouring out of their noses. They were the lucky ones, to have stuffed up noses. A few of the congregation had crapped their pants, judging by the stains on their clothes and the stench in the air.

Josie stared towards the blazing fires at the entrance as they wickedly licked the inside of the church. She glanced down the aisle in horror as her gaze fell upon the blue snakes writhing around at the foot of the raised pulpit, hissing and biting at each other. There was no way out.

She jumped when deep thunder echoed through the room and glanced up to see violent winds rip apart the inside of the chapel. Streaks of lighting shot around the small group of people huddled on the pulpit, making them scream and jerk in terror. Wailing pleas for God to help could be heard over the howling wind while the hurricane twisted its way up the church, about to engulf them.

Josie gasped at several loud stomps. The church shook violently before everything disappeared. The snakes vanished, the wind died down, the lightning stopped and the fire faded into nothing.

"Shit!" Dora cried as she walked back into her room and saw her carpet burning. She repeatedly stamped on the fire until the last ember turned to black ash.

"Crap," she said. *Dad's going to go ballistic over this.*

Dora sighed at the useless summoning circle, which was now a curled up, burnt mess. She threw herself onto her bed and lay on her stomach, staring at the black screen of her pink television. She pulled the remote control from beneath the mattress and pressed the power button on it.

Her TV was only allowed one network—her father's. She wasn't allowed to watch anything else. Thank Beelzebub her parents weren't net savvy, or she would be living in a religious bubble.

Since it was her bedtime, she knew the stupid show would be over soon. Sometimes the old black and white movies they showed late at night weren't too bad. Doris Day kicked ass in Calamity Jane.

The television flickered into life, and her dad's show appeared on the screen. People were wailing, crying and praising the Lord. *Aww shit, they didn't do another one of those miracle cures shows, did they?*

Dora's eyes widened as Molly Carmichael, the prim librarian from the main library, wandered in front of the camera mumbling incoherently. Molly turned her back to the camera and bowed to the pulpit. Dora's eyes widened more when she saw what she could only describe as effervescent shit stains decorating the back of Molly's pink tweed skirt. She watched Molly wander off camera, still mumbling random words like, 'snakes' and 'demons' as she disappeared from view.

For the first time ever, Dora found herself glued to her dad's show. *I can't believe I missed this.*

Her father finally came on screen as he pulled himself up off the floor. He clawed at the podium and dragged himself up, so his head appeared over it. He was shaking all over and had a few small cuts and gashes on his face. His hair looked like an oversized white afro hovering around his head. The priest's collar of his vestments hung limply down his neck in a white line.

"Dah …" He tried to speak, but his voice was so hoarse he only managed a sound. He was breathing hard. Judging by the murderous look in his eyes, she knew whatever he was about to say was not going to be good.

"Dohh …" He managed before taking a deep breath. He stared down at the podium for a moment in silent fury.

He eventually looked straight up into the camera. The moans and wails of parishioners were echoing behind him, through the microphone. "D-Do-Dora, I'm going to kill you!" Her father gasped into the camera before he passed out on the podium and slid to the floor.

Dora blinked at the screen. *Shit, what am I getting blamed for now?*

# 3

## INTO THE WARM AND STICKY

Kieron Lascher stopped chasing turquoise snakes when a burst of light exploded in the darkness a few feet away from him. He frowned and walked over to it. It was a hole ripped through the ether, a jagged tear of light in his dark and dismal world.

He reached out his hand and touched the shimmering light. It was warm and sticky. He pulled his hand back and glanced around him. There was no one around. Even the twittering hell spawn were up to no good elsewhere today. It wasn't surprising since it was only a couple of weeks until Judgment Day. Everyone was cramming for the finals.

Kieron knew he should be studying too. His father would eviscerate him if he failed this time. He had been revising all morning, trying to catch a snake for an experiment, but he had just ended up with several bites off the bloody things.

He tried not to let it bother him, but he was a failure

at being evil. Nothing ever worked out. He got the formulas right, but it just never turned out evil enough. If he failed his test this year, he would be expelled from Hell. Everyone knew what that meant. A fate worse than colonic irrigation—he would be exiled to Earth.

Kieron had never been to Earth. He'd been born in Hell, but he'd seen it through the various portals. He shuddered at the thought of it. He'd seen the monotonous work humans had to do; filing, spreadsheets ... homework! Humans were sorry creatures; they followed dreams of things they'd never have, and they were powerless in the world they lived in. He couldn't imagine anything worse. No, he had to pass the test this year—being exiled to Earth was not an option.

He tilted his head while he studied the tear of light. After a few minutes of contemplation, he decided the best plan was to fix it. It was dangerous leaving a gaping hole in the ether lying around like this. Someone might fall into it and hurt themselves.

He ran his fingers over the edges and encountered the warm sticky feeling again. *What kind of tear is it?* It pulsed as if it were alive. He'd never seen a portal like it, but there were a lot of lunatic demons practicing spells at this time of year. It was obviously a mistake because no talented warlock would create something so messy.

The wind howled around him in harsh, warm gusts. He glanced back and stared at the desolate horizon. *Are the volcanoes playing up again?* A vice-like grip clamped onto his wrist, which was still hovering over the tear in reality. He yelped when it tugged on his arm. The tear growled as it became a vortex, sucking things into it with howling winds and a terrifying force. Snakes and shrubbery shot past him as the growing hole consumed them. The ground shifted towards the portal, and the red sands of the barren landscape swirled around him. He attempted to scream but could only cough as the sand blew into his mouth.

He pulled back against the vacuum, trying to free himself from the portal, but the force was too powerful. He finally managed to cry out for help, but the sound was lost in the din. Using every muscle in his body, he tried to detach from the pulsing gash in reality. The power of the suction increased, lifting him off the ground before the portal pulled him into another realm.

Kieron squeezed his eyes shut as a blinding light flashed around him. His stomach leapt into his throat. The force of the pull flattened his cheeks to his skull. Every nerve in his body screamed in protest as gravity crushed it. He warily opened one eye, just in time to see the tear become a distant shadow. Flashes of bright lights sped past him. He crashed into something soft and expelled a shocked yelp of pain. Everything went dark as the portal closed.

He fought to suppress the urge to throw up while using his hands to search around in the dark. He could feel cloth draping over him and sharp painful blocks underneath him. He blindly explored his surroundings with his hands. The space was confined. He could feel the walls around him by simply stretching out his arms. He tried to control a bubble of panic when the thought of all those snakes being in here with him filled his mind.

His hand hit something on a string, a pendulum of some kind. He felt around for it in the darkness. It was wildly swinging around, but he caught it in his grasp on the third try. The heavy, metal object was hanging from twine. He tugged it to see if it would hold his weight. A bright light burst into the small room, and he found himself looking up the inside of a girl's dress. It would have been a pleasant experience had there been a girl inside the dress, but alas the dress was empty.

Something sharp dug into his backside, so he rooted around with his hands to pull the object out from beneath him. He stared at the shiny ruby slipper in his hand. The three-inch heel and pointed toe on the shoe answered some questions for him. *I'm in a witch's closet!*

Kieron pushed the clothes out of the way and got to his feet, ripping half of the dresses off their hangers in the process. He surveyed the inside of the closet before turning to face the slatted door. He inhaled a sharp breath when he stared through the gaps in the door and saw the witch.

She lay on a pink bed at the center of the room with her ebony hair twisted up in knots. Her blood-red lips pouted seductively at something she was watching. She was appealing to look at. Her long legs idly swung in the air behind her. She wore a pair of tiny red shorts and some kind of white tunic that had no sleeves. She was the first witch Kieron had ever seen, but his father had told him about them. They were all sexy little minxes with nasty tricks up their sleeves. He remembered seduction was their greatest trick, but he wasn't worried. He was pretty smooth with the ladies. He'd had the best tutors—succubae.

Kieron became aware of his own body swaying while he watched her legs swing back and forth behind her. *Hypnosis!* He realized and quickly averted his eyes up to the top of the closet, trying to calm his racing pulse. He refused to look at the witch and stared upwards. Piled on the shelf at the top of the closet were boxes and boxes of mysterious witch items. He tilted his head, trying to read the labels before reaching up to pull down the top box on the pile. It was red and white, the colors of blood and life. *It must be one of her darkest secrets.* It was labeled with one thick black word. He tried to pronounce the word in his mind. *Mono-Polly.* He didn't know this language, but it must be immensely powerful to have such colors on it. He took a deep breath and opened the box while his heart hammered.

Inside was an odd-looking ritual board. *What kind of casting can you do with this?* It had places on it with haunting names like 'Marylebone Station' and 'The Strand'. There were strange tarot cards called 'Chance' and 'Community Chest'. He recognized small silver ritual symbols of pagan items like the iron and the boot, but they were mixed in with symbols he hadn't seen before. He gasped when he picked up the small icon of a dog, dropping the box in shock. *What kind of monster is this witch? She'd cast upon a helpless hound.*

He nearly screamed when he looked through the slats in the door and saw her staring straight at him. She sat up on the bed and began making her way over to the closet. He inwardly cursed himself for making such a racket when he dropped the box.

He found his eyes drawn to her ample bosom when she stood up. *Think clean thoughts, think clean thoughts,* he told himself. *This minx will not turn me into her demon slave, no matter how bouncy they look. Er, she looks.*

He froze, overcome with a feeling of helplessness when she walked towards the door, reaching for the handle.

Her chamber door burst open, and a deranged holy man with wild white hair stormed into the room. He carried a crucifix in one hand and a bag of salt in the other.

Kieron involuntarily hissed as the witch spun around to face the man.

He instinctively glanced down, his eyes drawn to her ass.

"BACK DEMON!" Dora forgot about the noise in her closet as she spun around to face her father. He held a crucifix in front of him and appeared slightly crazed. His vestments were ripped and dirty, his hair was sticking out in a wild afro, and the insane gleam in his eyes could only mean one thing—exorcism time.

Dora backed away from him to the center of the room. "Dad, come on. Whatever I did, I didn't mean it," she said, holding her hands up in an attempt to placate him.

"SILENCE DEMON!" He bellowed before waving his cross at her.

"Oh, for fuc—ahhh …" Dora yawned in mid-argument. *Screw it, I can't be bothered. Just entertain his insanity, and you'll get to bed faster.*

She obediently stood in the center of the room while watching her father pour a circle of salt onto the floor around her. He shouted scripture at her, causing her to yawn again. Through bleary eyes, she studied him as he rushed to the wall and began nailing crosses to it around the doorframe. Sweat poured down his red face while he hammered the last cross into the wall.

He turned towards her, his knuckles turning white as he tightly gripped the bag of salt. "This will hold you, demon. Tomorrow you shall be sent back to Hell."

"Okay, Dad." Dora rubbed her eyes with her fists, hoping he would bugger off soon, so she could go back to bed.

Her father lined the window ledge with salt, then the doorway before carefully stepping over it and leaving the room. "You'll burn for your sins." He told her before he closed the door.

"Okie dokie." She agreed as the door slammed shut. She shook her head at the insanity of her life.

Just before she stepped out of the circle, the door to her closet burst open. An attractive blond-haired boy with bright blue eyes fell through the door. He wore a swashbuckler's shirt and tight leather pants. "Don't worry, Minx-witch. I shall save you!" he cried.

Dora gasped and swung her fist out at the strange boy. Her fist made a solid connection with his jaw and sent him flipping over face first onto the floor. She looked down at his unconscious body and sighed. "Okay, if you must." She had a feeling it was going to be a long night.

## 4

### WITCHES AND BITCHES

D ora studied the unconscious guy sprawled face down on her puce carpet. He was gorgeous even with his mouth hanging open and a bit of drool coming out of it. He had high cheekbones, a strong jawline, smooth tanned skin, broad shoulders and a perfect ass. She inclined her head sideways and checked out his backside. He was wearing a pair of tight brown leather pants. It was almost hypnotic watching his buttocks randomly flex.

She opened the leather pouch she had stolen from his belt. It was the closest thing he had to a wallet. It didn't contain money or any kind of identification, only a range of colorful gems. Given his choice of clothing and the contents of his pouch, she could only assume he was a crazy pirate. *That makes no sense. What would a pirate be doing in Berkville?*

The boy groaned, and she sighed with relief. She was glad she hadn't done any serious damage to him. He rolled over onto his back and gazed up at her with sleepy eyes. Little bursts of electricity tingled all over her body when his bright blue eyes scanned her from head to toe in lazy appreciation.

He smiled as he stretched his arms across the carpet, arching his back in the process. He paused when his fingers trailed over the circle of salt beside him. He briefly glanced at the salt and then back to Dora. His eyes widened in an instant, and his smile slipped. He jumped up yelping and frantically searching the room for something. "Oww! It burns, it burns," he cried, shaking his hand as if trying to get the grains of salt off it.

"What does?" She ran to his side to try and help, but he pushed her away during his desperate search of her room.

"Wash it off, the salt. Please, wash it off." He begged as he wildly waved his hand around.

Dora snatched his hand out of the air, tightly gripping his wrist while she examined it. His palm was large and masculine compared to her small hands. The skin was smooth and tanned like the rest of him, but there wasn't a mark on it. It certainly wasn't burning. "It's not burning," she said as she showed him it.

He stopped dancing around like a lunatic and glanced down, peering at his hand in awe. Confusion furrowed his brow as she brushed the grains of salt off his palm.

"It's supposed to be burning." He peered up, and their eyes locked.

Her skin heated up, and a shiver trembled up her back. "Umm, why?" She attempted to appear unaffected by his close proximity.

"Because it's salt," he said, implying she should know what he meant.

Dora didn't know what to make of him. She just stared at him.

"Minx-witch, you should know these things." He told her.

"Who?" she asked. Why did he keep calling her that? His warm fingers massaged her hand before they traveled up to her wrist and arm.

"Okay, enough games," he said with defeat in his tone, but his eyes were sparkling with something else. "You win."

"Wha—" She didn't finish as he pulled her into his arms and kissed her. His hard body pressed against her, and his warm hands roamed up her back. She almost melted into his wicked kisses—almost.

Dora pushed him away. "What the hell do you think you're doing?"

"Becoming your willing slave." He winked at her and rested his hands on her hips.

Her heart did a little backflip. "Fine. Clean my room," she replied. *Heart, behave yourself. Who the hell is this guy?*

"Uh, I'm not that kind of slave. That's not my purpose."

"Your purpose? What the hell were you doing in my closet? Who are you?" She stepped back and untangled herself from his embrace in case he attacked her again. She could handle many things; violence, robbery even religious zealots, but someone being nice to her and kissing her was a whole new experience.

"Oh, how rude of me." He dipped his head in a short bow before raising her hand to his lips and kissing it. "Let me introduce myself. I am Lord Kieron D. Lascher."

Dora snatched her hand back before he kissed anything else and caused her brain to shrink. "What does the 'D' stand for?"

"Oh, er, Derek," he mumbled. "And you are?"

"Derek?" She expelled a surprised giggle.

"It means ruler." He appeared offended. "What's your name, Minx-witch?" he snapped.

"Dora Carridine."

"Hmm, and *you* mock my name?" Kieron pouted at her.

"Sorry," she mumbled, laughing. "It was fun—wait. Who the hell are you, and what were you doing in my closet?  Did Dad put you in there?"

"Does your father often put young men in your closet late at night?" Kieron asked. He appeared genuinely curious.

"Er, not so far, but you never know with him."

"I cannot confirm who put me in your closet, for I do not know. But I was ripped from my home and brought here for a reason. The longer I am here, the more I realize that it was the fates that sent me." He studied her for a moment. "I believe I have been sent here for you. In fact, I am sure of it."

The words made something inside Dora heat up, and a shiver trembled through her body. Maybe it was because

CLAIRE CHILTON

he looked so honorable and hot when he said it. Also, what girl wouldn't love a guy that fate sent to her?

"What makes you think that?" she asked.

"You clearly need saving. It is simply a question of from what?" He slowly walked around her. "You are a minx-witch who is trapped in a tower by an evil holy man. Perhaps I am to save you from him?"

He'd been standing behind her for a while. She wondered what he was doing back there, so she spun around and caught him staring at the place her ass had been a few moments earlier. She scowled at him.

"Clearly you are also lacking in your skills as a minx if your kisses are anything to go by. Perhaps my duty is to teach you seduction." He grinned as he leapt at her, knocking her onto the bed and pinning her down by the wrists. "Would you like that?"

Dora acted on instinct. She kneed him in the balls as hard as she could before pushing him off her.

He rolled sideways onto the bed and curled up in agony. "Why would you do that?" he cried. "What kind of demon-witch are you?"

"One who is perfectly capable of taking care of herself," she replied as she got off the bed and picked up a heavy vase. "Try that again, and I'll knock you senseless—again!"

He held up his hands in submission and sat up on the bed. "So, why am I here? Why else would I be here if not to help you?" He appeared to be genuinely confused.

"Where did you come from?" she asked. She needed to know who this guy was. All she knew so far was he used old-fashioned words, and he was a bit of a perv.

"Hell," he said, waving his hand in the air as if to brush the question away. "Sinner's Hall, the fifth level."

Dora stared at him in awe. "Hell? Y-y-you're a demon?"

"Obviously," he said, appearing a bit upset that she hadn't already known that. "Can't you tell by my evil ways?"

"Well, er, no." She studied his handsome face and attractive body. "Aren't demons supposed to have horns?"

"Only hell spawn have them on the outside. The main demons are just—"

"Horny?" She cut in.

Kieron flashed a wicked grin.

Dora shook her head. "I can't believe I ask for a demon lord, and I get *you*."

"Hey! I am a demon lord." He shot her an annoyed glance. "A big evil one, a master of destruction ..."

She peered in her closet. "Dress destruction?"

"That wasn't my fault."

"Uh huh, how exactly are *you* evil? You came here to save me!"

"And to defile you, of course." He defended his evil ways.

"Okay, so ... I summoned you. That makes you my bitch, right?"

"I do not know that term." He sounded confused.

"Bitch? It means slave or servant, but in a good and manly way." Dora grinned.

"Ah, I see. Yes Minx-witch-Dora, I am your bitch."

She stifled a giggle. "Right then, *My Bitch*, there will be no defiling of me, and you will do as I command, understand?"

"Not even a little bit of defiling?" A disappointed expression appeared on his face.

"No, none at all."

"Evildoing?" His blue eyes shone with hope.

"There probably will be some evildoing." She admitted.

"Okay, that sounds good." Kieron agreed.

"Good. Now, I'm tired. It's been a really long day, so I'm going to go to bed, and I suggest you do the same." She told him before she climbed into bed and hugged her pillow.

The bed trembled as he got off it, and she snuggled under her blanket. The bed bounced as a weight landed on it. A hot body pressed against her back, and a strong masculine arm snaked around her waist.

"Bitch."

"Yes, my minx." His hot breath warmed the back of her neck.

"What are you doing?"

"Sleeping."

"Not in my bed."

"Oh come on! What's a shared bed between a master and their minion?"

Dora rolled over and pushed him off the bed with as much force as she could muster.

"Fine." He snapped, pushing himself off the floor. "I'll sleep in the closet."

"Good bitch," she said, stifling a laugh as he stomped over to the closet, walked into it and slammed the door shut behind him.

After a few minutes, she began to worry about Kieron. *There isn't enough room in the closet for him to lie down.* With a sigh, she climbed out of bed and walked over to the closet door, deciding he'd be fine with a sleeping bag on the floor, instead.

Dora opened the door while trying to think of the best way to suggest he should sleep on her floor. She blinked at the scene inside her closet. Kieron lay on a round king-sized waterbed adorned with red silk sheets and an array of opulent pillows and blankets. The closet had been transformed into a large room with everything from a minibar to a couch fitting comfortably inside it.

He glanced up at her with a devilish grin. "I knew you'd change your mind, my frisky little minx. There's room for two." He winked.

"Bitch," she said before slamming the door on him. She walked away from the closet and climbed back into her pink bed, hugging her blanket and trying not to think about devilish demons.

*Sleep,* she told herself. *Maybe when I wake up the world will be sane again.*

# 5

## RITUALE ROMANUM

Dora idly spun around in her computer chair while her mother sprinkled a circle of salt around her. She tugged on the ropes binding her wrists to the chair arms and sighed. It was exorcism time.

Her father walked around the room holding his e-copy of the Rituale Romanum and a crucifix in his hands.

"Mom, this is getting ridiculous. You know it's me." She pleaded with her mother, who was the least insane parent.

"It's the only way to help you, Dora." Her mother refused to look her in the eye.

"I've got exams coming up soon. I need to go to school to pass those. Keeping me prisoner in here is not going to help my GPA."

Finally, her mother glanced at her as if considering the possibility that she might actually graduate one day. Josie turned to Dora's father. "She probably should be at school today."

"You think we should let this *thing* defile another child at the school?" Theodore snapped at Josie. He turned to Dora. "Do you think me foolish demon?"

"I'm not a fucking demon!" Dora snapped, pulling against the ropes.

"Such obscene language coming from my baby's lips." Her mother gasped and stood back, holding her hand to her mouth in shock. "No child of mine would use such words."

"Shit." Dora knew she'd just blown her chances of getting out of this.

Her father nodded at her mother and opened his book. Well, it wasn't actually a book. It was a printout in a clear plastic binder.

Dora slumped in her chair and pouted at him.

He cleared his throat and began reading from the folder in a slow droning voice. "Exorcizamus te, omnis immundus spiritus—"

"Aww, come on! This is going to take hours. Read faster." Dora complained.

Her father scowled at her before continuing in the same drone. "Omnis satanica potestas, omnis incursion infernalis adversarii, omnis legio, omnis congregatio et secta diabolica—"

"Do you actually know what any of that means?" Dora interrupted.

Her mother splashed her face with holy water in reply. Dora blinked, feeling cold-water drip down her face and onto her chest. "Great! Now I'll have to curl my hair again."

29

"Ergo draco maledicte et omnis legio diabolica adjuramus te." Her father chanted.

Panic twisted in Dora's stomach when she heard a hiss from behind her closet door. Kieron must have woken up. She struggled with the rope around her wrists. She would be in deep shit if they found Kieron. "Okay, I'm cured," she cried. "Mommy, I can't feel the demon anymore." She attempted to look innocent and saved.

"Deceitful demon, we know your lies," her father said. "I will finish this ritual and send you back to Hell."

"Aww shit. Are you kidding me? That's going to take ages."

"Cessa decipere humanas creaturas, eisque aeternae Perditionis venenum propinare." Her father continued with renewed vigor.

Dora heard a hiss from her closet door again. She coughed loudly to cover it up.

"It's working, Theodore!" her mother cried. "The demon is coming out. Keep going."

"Vade, Satana, inventor et magister omnis fallaciae, hostis humanae salutis. Humiliare sub potenti manu dei, contremisce et effuge, invocato a nobis sancto et terribili nomine, quem inferi tremunt."

Dora's eyes widened as she saw the handle on her closet begin to turn. "Kieron, no!" she shouted. "I command you to stay out."

"Yes demon, stay out of my daughter," her mother shouted, and she threw more holy water in Dora's face.

Dora blinked and sniffed. "You're just going to keep doing that, aren't you? Regardless of how wet I get."

Her mother splashed a cup full of holy water in Dora's face as a reply. Her hair, face and chest were now drenched in icy water. Cold dribbles ran down her cheeks and splashed onto her collarbone. She exhaled a resigned sigh. "I'll take that as a yes."

"Ab insidiis diaboli, libera nos, Domine. Ut Ecclesiam tuam secura tibi facias libertate servire te rogamus, audi nos." Her father continued, his voice thankfully rising in volume and drowning out the sounds of a struggle inside her closet.

*Is this hurting Kieron?* She worried.

"Ut inimicos sanctae Ecclesiae humiliare digneris, te rogamus, audi nos. Terribilis Deus ..." Her father paused. "Er, Josie dear, did you fill up the printer with new ink?"

"Yes, last week. They had Cyan on offer at PC World, so I stocked up on it," her mother replied.

"Did you put the ink in the printer?"

"Hmm? I think so."

"So, the Roman Catholic exorcism ritual ends with the words 'God is frightening'?" Dora's father did not appear convinced.

While watching her mother ponder the question, Dora realized it was now or never. If she wanted to help Kieron, it would require an Oscar winning performance, right now.

"ARRGHHHH!" She arched violently in her chair and made her legs and arms sporadically twitch. "IT BURNS!" she growled from the back of her throat. It was actually her 'Oscar from Sesame Street' impression, but it was convincing enough.

"It must do, Theodore. Look! It's working." Josie sounded overjoyed.

Dora shuddered and cried out a few random Latin words before limply slumping in her chair. She peeked out at them with one eye. Her mother was beaming, and her father was almost smiling. He'd put down the binder and was heading towards her. She realized the struggling sounds in her closet had ceased too.

Her mother began untying her, but her father stopped her. "We must be certain this new ritual worked before we release her." He told his wife.

Dora snapped her eye shut when her father leaned over her. Her head tilted upwards as he lifted her chin with his fingers.

"Dora," he said in a soft voice.

She slowly opened her eyes as if waking from a deep sleep. "Is it gone Father? Am I safe now?" She tried to imagine what a nice girl would say. It was the toughest acting she'd ever done.

"Yes Dora, you're safe now. How do you feel?" her father asked.

"Strange Father, as if I've been gone for a very long time." She fluttered her eyelashes for effect.

"You have, my child, but it is okay. You're safe."

*Oh, I'm gonna barf if I need to keep up this crap for much longer.*

"I should pray to God and thank him." She hoped they'd untie her soon, and those appeared to have been the magic words.

"Yes Dora, that's right." Her father quickly untied

her wrists and released her from the chair. "Come, let us do that now." He tried to guide her out of the room with him.

*Like hell!*

"I feel the need to pray to God on my own, Father. To ask for forgiveness by myself. After all, I can't ask others to take on my responsibilities and er stuff, can I?" She found it increasingly difficult to keep up the act now she was free of her chair.

"I understand, and you are right child." Her father hugged her, and for a brief second it was almost as if she had a normal father. "Come Josie. Let us leave Dora to her prayers. She has so much sin to repent for."

The parental moment vanished when she heard that. She watched her parents head towards the door while grinding her teeth to stop herself from saying what she really thought.

"Honey, I'm so glad you're okay. We can give you confession tomorrow and buy you nicer clothes," her mother said when she paused in the doorway.

Dora walked to the door and flashed a sweet smile before she shut the door in her mother's face and locked it. "Yeah, that'll fuckin' happen."

She rushed to the closet and swung open the door to check on Kieron. He lay in a heap on the floor of his plush red room. Her eyes widened when she noticed he appeared to be tied up in a pair of her stockings and was gagged by one of her bras. "What the hell?" She pulled the bra out of his mouth and scowled at him. "Were you trying to eat my underwear?"

"What? No! It attacked me," Kieron said.

"My bra attacked you?"

"Yes, I was just listening at the door to the holy man hurting you. I was about to come to your rescue, but he spelled your underwear so it attacked me!"

She reached down to untie him. "Is that all that happened? They used the exorcism ritual, and all it did was made you eat bra?"

"I know, right? I'd have expected it to make me eat pants or something instead," he said with an innocent expression on his face.

Dora snorted laughing. "Yeah, that's what I was worrying about," she said as she finished untying him from her stockings and helped him up off the floor.

Kieron rubbed his wrists, watching her with a concerned frown. "What did they do to you, Minx-witch?"

"Ah, nothing. Just stupid parent crap." She shrugged. But in all honesty, she felt attacked and unsafe in her own home, just like always.

"I don't like stupid parents." He growled and pulled her into a hug. This hug was so different from the ones her father gave her. It was close, comforting and real.

"No, neither do I." She agreed, enjoying the warmth of his body against hers.

He rubbed her back and held her close for quite some time. After a while, she realized it was the first time she'd ever enjoyed a hug.

"Kieron?"

"Yes, my minx?"

"What are you thinking about?"

"You naked." His breath blew against her hair.

"Are you shitting me?" She angrily pushed him away. "Men!"

"What?" he asked with confusion in his eyes. "It was the truth."

She shook her head and stormed back to her own room, slamming the closet door behind her. She threw herself face first onto her bed and hugged her pillow. A few tears might have escaped from her eyes, but she refused to acknowledge them. *People suck!*

# STRANGE MAGIC

Kieron quietly opened the door and watched his minx-witch on her bed. There was something wrong with her. She was volatile and not at all sexy right now. She was making strange sniffling noises and confusing him with hiccups.

"Minx-witch, I need to help you. They have cast some kind of spell on you, I think. You are not working properly." He smiled. She should understand that.

A pink fluffy pillow whapped him across the face, and he sighed.

"Dora-minx, you cannot go on like this. It's bad for your health and quite unattractive." He ducked as an alarm clock flew at him from Dora's bedside.

"Stop throwing things at me!" he shouted.

"Go away." Dora's muffled reply came from somewhere inside her pillow.

"Where?" he asked, puzzled.

"Anywhere!"

He shook his head and perched on the side of the bed. "Silly Minx-witch, there is no place called *anywhere*. I know. I checked."

"Just leave me alone." Her muffled voice replied.

"Now is not a good time to be alone, Dora-minx. You have been spelled." He reached across her and attempted to roll her over, so she would be facing him. "Come on. Let me see what they have done to you. There's no need to hide. Even the most powerful witches suffer at the hands of imbeciles, sometimes."

Dora struggled with him for a little while before eventually rolling over and looking at him.

He jumped back in shock. "By the Devil's fucknuts, what have they done to you?"

Black tears were rolling down her face in streaks. Her eyes were red, but not as red as her nose that was glowing so much it was shiny and appeared swollen. She repeatedly sniffed and hiccupped.

"What is this awful spell? Your beautiful face, what destruction is this upon it?" He panicked. He had never seen this kind of ugliness before. Boils and warts sure, he'd seen those. But to make her eyes bleed black, what sorcery was this? "I don't know what to do, Minx-witch. Do you know what this is?" he asked. "What spell cast did they use? Did you see the book?"

"It's okay, Kieron." She smiled. Although she was still quite unattractive, he was pleased she wasn't in pain. "I know how to fix this."

"What can I do to help?" he asked.

"Pass me the box of tissues." She told him.

He leapt across the room and snatched the tissues from the top of her dresser. He knelt beside her, holding the tissues out to her. He was anxious for her face to be restored to its former beauty. This curse was causing him to feel something awful inside, and he didn't like the feeling.

He watched her wipe her eyes with the magic tissues before blowing her nose on another tissue. It was a miraculous thing to watch as her face transformed before him to become pretty again. Her eyes were still a little red, but her nose appeared less swollen now. Her face was almost back to normal.

Kieron sighed with relief. "I must learn more about these new curses and cures, my Minx. How can I protect you if not?"

"You don't have to protect me, Kieron. I'm fine." Dora-minx's voice was still shaky. The curse must have taken a lot out of her. He summoned her heart's desire; a large tub of cookies and cream Hagen Daz and a spoon. He offered her them.

A smile lit up her face when she accepted his gift. "How did you do that?" The delight in her voice made him happy.

"It is easy, Dora-minx. I find it in the world and bring it here."

Dora paused opening the ice cream. "You mean you took it from someone else?"

"Of course, but he was a fat kid who had bullied it from another kid in the mall. He'll do well in Hell that boy, mark my words."

"What about the first kid who had it stolen from him by the fat kid?"

"Oh, I think he's cursed. He has the same look on his face that you had a few minutes ago. Should I send him some tissues?"

"No, send him this ice cream back," she said. "It will help him."

"But, what about you, do you not need the ice cream?" He tilted his head to one side feeling puzzled.

"No. Er, just trust me on this one." She smiled again, and it made him happy again. He was supposed to go to the family barbeque in Hell tonight, but he really wanted to stay here with Dora instead.

"As you command, Minx-witch," he said. He snapped his fingers and sent the ice cream back to the cursed kid. He curiously watched the child in his mind. Dora-minx was right. The boy's curse lifted when the ice cream reappeared.

*What strange magic is this?*

"Dora-minx, I have decided to stay with you for the time being. I think you need my help, and I can learn more about your world while I am here."

"Can you leave when you want to?" She frowned at him.

"Of course, I am all powerful."

"I thought once you'd been summoned, you'd be stuck here."

"No." He pondered the question. Portals usually worked both ways. "I can just click my fingers and choose where I am. Look …" He clicked his fingers and nothing

39

happened.

Dora raised an eyebrow.

He frowned and clicked his fingers. Nothing happened again. He laughed. "I must have done it wrong, one second." He shook his hand and clicked his fingers again. "It was working a minute ago, I swear."

"I don't think you can go back unless you're sent back," she said.

"You mean I-I—I really am your bitch?" A bubble of panic swelled in his throat.

"Er, I'm not sure, but I think you need a spell to go back."

"Fucknuts," he muttered.

"Don't worry, we'll figure it out." She reassured him.

Kieron stood up and paced around the room feeling an anxious knot tightening in his stomach. "No, you don't understand."

"What do you mean?" Dora-minx looked very pretty when she worried.

He sighed and shook his head. "I cannot miss Judgment Day. I have to get back in time."

"When is it and what happens if you don't?"

"In thirteen days, and very bad things will happen," he said in a dark tone.

"What kind of things?"

"My father will come to get me."

# FIREKNACKERS

**D**ora thought about Kieron's father as she filled a bag with supplies from the kitchen cupboards. She and Kieron had talked all day in her room about it, and in all honesty, his father sounded like a bigger asshole than her own did. Being eviscerated for missing a barbeque was definitely child abuse.

Hunger had eventually grumbled in both their bellies, so she had decided to sneak downstairs for supplies.

She checked her bag. *Twinkies-check, soda-check, jerky-check. What else do we need?* She wondered while browsing the choice of cakes and candy.

Dora didn't realize anyone was behind her until a pair of strong arms grabbed her. "DEMON!" Her father roared.

"Aww shit, not again." She struggled to get out of his reach.

"Josie, come in here. Check what she's stealing," her father shouted into the living room.

Her mother rushed into the room with her blond hair bouncing around in rollers. "Oh no, Theodore, didn't it work?" her mother cried.

"Alas no my dear, our daughter is truly lost," her father replied. "Check her bag. See what the demon was taking from us."

Josie ripped the bag out of Dora's hands and tipped it out onto the floor. Dora groaned. It was her school bag— it had all of her supplies in it.

Twinkies, soda and jerky fell out first followed by bloodroot, her grimoire, sage and some black candles. "I can explain that," Dora said.

"Witchcraft!" her father bellowed.

"Well, yes. I suppose you could call it that. I mean, it's almost science in some ways. You know, mixing chemicals and things. Like homework," she added with a hopeful smile.

"Demon worship!" Her father shook her so hard her teeth rattled.

"I'm not really into the worshipping—you might have noticed. It's more experimenting." She winced. This was not going to end well.

"There is only one solution to this, Josie." Her father sounded sad.

"I know." Her mother lowered her head. "I'll call the council." She walked out of the room crying.

"The council?" Dora asked.

Her father said nothing as he marched her out of the kitchen.

Dora's breath exploded out of her lungs when she landed in a heap on her bedroom floor. She scowled at her father, who was closing the door behind him after throwing her into the room. She inhaled sharply when she heard a loud clunk of her father locking the bolt on the other side of the door. *What's he going to do to me this time, keep me prisoner?*

She sat up on the floor and glanced around the room, looking for Kieron. She frowned when she couldn't see him and called out his name.

Kieron peeked out of the closet and widened his eyes at her. "What happened, Dora-minx?" he said, rushing over to help her up.

"I got caught stealing Twinkies. I think they figured out I'm a witch." She glanced at the door, frowning with worry.

"Did they not already know you were a witch?"

"No, I—I don't think they did. I think they thought I was possessed by a demon all this time."

Kieron laughed at the idea. "Demon possession is such a myth, as if we'd choose a helpless human to ride around the world in."

"Why wouldn't you?" she asked as her curiosity overrode her concern.

"Would you steal a bicycle if you owned a Ferrari?"

"Fair point."

"So, what spell do they cast on witches?" he asked.

"Maybe I'll get into your pants this time?"

Dora aimed a punch at him, and he held up his hands in surrender.

"I mean be attacked by them!"

She lowered her fist. "I don't know what they do to witches, but it's the first time they've put the bolt on the outside of my door."

"That's not a good sign." He studied the door for a moment. "I can open it, you know."

"Yeah I know, but I think we're better off waiting to see what happens for now. Anyway, we've got nowhere else to go." She thought about it all. *Who are the council?* Her stomach interrupted her thoughts as it rumbled with hunger. She hadn't eaten anything yet today. "What are we going to do about food?"

"Not a problem." He winked, and her bag full of snacks materialized on the carpet.

"Maybe you are here to save me, after all," she muttered as she grabbed a Twinkie and devoured it. Kieron sank to the floor opposite her and helped himself to one too.

"All the signs are pointing that way," he replied, after swallowing his Twinkie in one bite. He stretched out on the fluffy pink carpet like a languid cat and stared up at the ceiling as if deep in thought.

"Well, I guess we've got a lot of time to kill. Tell me about Hell." Dora folded her legs beneath her, sitting cross-legged on the floor. She rested her elbows on her knees and her head in her hands in preparation of a good story. She liked listening to Kieron's stories about Hell. It almost sounded like a fun place.

Kieron rolled onto his side and propped himself up on his elbow. He flashed a smile that made her pulse race. She tightened her stomach muscles and her skin heated up under his intense gaze. He appeared oblivious to the effect he had on her and nodded. "In the third level of Hell there are amusement parks, all of them. Where the rollercoasters make you so sick, you know you've been to DisneyLevel if you've vomited on Mickey Mouse's head." He grinned at the memories. "The guy in the mouse suit is the one in Hell there."

Dora laughed. "That's so gross."

"Yes." He nodded. "Gross is good in Hell."

She was about to ask more when a loud thud made her jump as something hard hit her window. She and Kieron both locked eyes for a moment before rushing to the window to see what had hit it.

Dora brushed aside the curtain and gasped when she saw the street below. Hundreds of people were standing on the front lawn of the church, staring up at her window. It looked as if half the town was down there. She flinched as another rock bounced off the glass near her face.

"What the hell?" She noticed the people on the lawn were chanting something, but she couldn't hear what they were saying through the double-glazing. She cracked open the window enough to let the sound in, but not enough to let the rocks in.

"Witch, witch, kill the bitch!" The voices of the people below chanted.

"Do you think they mean me?" she asked Kieron.

"I think they mean for *you* to kill me," he replied. "Witch." He pointed to Dora. "Kill the bitch." He pointed to himself. "You're not going to kill me are you, Dora-minx?"

"No, don't be silly. I don't think they know you're my bitch. I think they're calling me a bitch and are suggesting I should be killed."

She stared out of the window again and narrowed her eyes. "Traitorous old bats!" she cried.

"What is it?" Kieron asked.

"The fucking Wiccans are there! They're witches too—bloody hypocrites." Her face heated up as it flushed in anger.

A devilish grin grew on Kieron's face. He mumbled something under his breath before wiggling his fingers at the Wicca group on the lawn. Dora snorted with laughter when their pants ignited in a burst of flames. They screamed while struggling out of their fiery underwear in public.

"Ah, there's nothing like burnt genitals in the morning." He inhaled, flashing an evil grin.

Dora burst out laughing. "You need to show me that spell."

Kieron winked. "I will. It's called Fireknackers."

While they both stared down at the angry mob below, she considered her options. She realized Kieron must have been having similar thoughts when he broke the silence. "I think we need to get out of here."

"And go where?" she asked. "I'm sure I can sort this out. It's just a misunderstanding, right?"

"I dunno. Everything I learned about humans implies when they group together they become a pain in the ass and very, very stupid. Kind of like a can of condensed moron that's about to explode." He studied the people on the lawn before shooting Dora a thoughtful glance. "Why don't you come to Hell with me? It's nice there. You'd fit in, I reckon. It's not as if the people here appreciate your talents."

She was tempted. It was kinda lame here, and she trusted Kieron. No matter how bad Hell was, she wouldn't be alone there, which was an improvement on this life. She sighed. *What about my parents?* They were messed up, sure, but she couldn't just abandon them. They'd never get over it.

Another rock hit the window and a crack appeared in the glass. She took a step back. "I better see if I can sort this out first." She smiled at Kieron. "But thank you."

Kieron frowned at the people below. "I don't think there will be an easy fix for this, Dora-minx. People are often stupid and evil. It is why Hell is so full of them."

# BURN BABY BURN

Dora jumped when there was a loud knock at her door. She silently motioned for Kieron to go in the closet by waving him away with her hands. She waited a few seconds until he was out of sight before inhaling a deep breath and opening the door with a smile. She jumped back to avoid being hit in the face by the door when it was forcefully shoved open. Her father and three other men rushed into the room and grabbed her. She attempted to scream, but Principal Jackson's sweaty hand covered her mouth.

Dora glared at her captors, recognizing all of them. The men restraining her were her father, Police Chief Dawson, Principal Jackson and Mayor Taylor. *This must be the council*, she realized. *The council members are all from the fucking rotary club!*

As they dragged her out of the room, she panicked. She kicked and tried to scream, but they restrained her in an iron grip. She struggled and jerked, but quickly discovered there was no getting away from them. Her pulse raced, and her heart beat so loudly she was surprised no one else could hear it. She felt as if she'd had the air knocked out of her lungs and found it difficult to breathe. She tried to think rationally, but her mind was a mess. *What the hell is going on?*

After a mild panic attack, she realized they were planning to take her out of the building when she noticed the muddy boots they all wore. She realized she had a much better chance of getting away from them if she walked on her own legs, instead of them carrying her. She forced herself to calm down and stop struggling.

The group stopped at the top of the narrow staircase, which led down to the ground floor. They set her on her feet, just as she'd hoped they would.

"We should read her, her rights," Dora's father said.

Mayor Taylor nodded. "You're right, Theodore. We are remiss in not doing so earlier."

"Don't make a sound, witch, or you'll regret it." Principal Jackson hissed in her ear before he removed his hand from her mouth.

"What the fuck is going on?" Dora shouted.

Principal Jackson scowled at her before brushing his lank gray hair out of his icy blue eyes. Her father shook his head at her and exhaled a disappointed sigh.

"Ahem." The mayor cleared his throat.

She glanced at Mayor Taylor. He smoothed his black mustache with shaking fingers as a nervous smile appeared on his usually red jovial face. "Dora Carridine, you are being arrested under suspicion of being a witch. You have been accused of consorting with demons and committing dark crimes against humanity. You will be taken from this place to trial, where you will be judged. Do you understand?"

"Can I call my lawyer?" Dora asked.

The mayor and her father glanced at each other, appearing confused. The mayor held up his hand to indicate she should wait a moment before the two men huddled together whispering for a few minutes.

Meanwhile, Police Chief Dawson grabbed her wrists and handcuffed her hands behind her back.

After a lot of nodding and shaking of heads, the mayor and her father came back to the group.

"You will be represented legally by the word of God," Mayor Taylor said.

"Are you shitting me? An invisible being is going to be my fucking lawyer?" Dora cried, trying to get her hands out of the cuffs.

"You have the right to remain silen—" Chief Dawson began.

"No thanks" She cut in.

"Anything you say will be, er …"

"Ignored?"

"Enough!" Principal Jackson pushed her towards the stairs. "She's not a bank robber. She's an instrument of the devil, an evil witch. Let's get on with this."

Dora glanced back at him and shivered when she noticed a wild gleam of insanity in his eyes.

After she realized she couldn't rationalize with these lunatics, she walked down the stairs flanked on either side by walls, hoping an opportunity to escape would present itself. Her mind was reeling, but her common sense told her to be patient. With Chief Dawson in front of her and the rest of the group behind her, she was trapped on the staircase. She watched Chief Dawson's back as he ambled down the stairs. Like all the other men, he was in his late forties or early fifties. He was short and stocky with large meaty arms, and his dark hair was styled in a buzz cut. She glanced back at her father, wondering if he would save her. But his expression was resolute and cold, showing no emotion.

She walked calmly through the church towards the entrance. Cool on the outside, but inside her heart was hammering. Fear and panic pooled in the back of her throat. *What are they going to do to me?*

They led her through the large double doors of the church and on to the front lawn. Crowds of people had gathered on the lawn. At least half the population of the small town of Berkville was there, all baying for blood— hers.

The noise was deafening, and the angry mob was a terrifying sight. Panic turned to debilitating fear, which caused her to freeze in terror when she saw the structure ahead of her. A pyre had appeared on the end of their front lawn. It was a bonfire with a thick post driven through the center of it. She realized Kieron had been right. People grouped together were morons, and these morons were going to try to burn her alive. *Oh shit, oh shit, oh shit!*

Hands behind her pushed her forward, towards the

51

pyre. She realized her chance of escaping was now or never. "Fuck this," she muttered as she made a run for it. Her hands cuffed behind her back slowed her down, but she pumped her legs as fast as they would run, making a beeline towards the pyre. She planned on running around the bonfire to avoid the crowds of people on either side of her. Hands tried to grab her as she ran past them, clawing at her clothes as she dodged by. She could hear the heavy footsteps of the four council members pounding on the garden path behind her, gaining on her. She hitched her breath in fear, feeling as if her heart was going to burst out of her chest.

A brief glance back caused another tremor of fear to shiver down her spine. All she could see was the angry face of her father running after her. She stumbled and fell when she plowed into someone in her way. She hit the ground hard when they grabbed her and took her down with them. *No, no, no!*

Dora stared up into her mother's hazel eyes as she held her down. "Please, Mom." She begged before strong hands pulled her to her feet and held her captive. Her mother averted her eyes and didn't say a word.

Something in Dora broke at that moment. Some part of her could no longer forgive the things they'd done to her. It was the worst kind of betrayal. The crowds of people were a blur around her, all crying out for her to burn.

Chief Dawson took off her handcuffs, but it was her father who tied her to the post at the center of the pyre. His face set in steely determination as he bound the rope around her several times.

She saw Mrs. Smiggins helping her mother off the ground, patting her on the back as if offering her some kind of twisted praise. She heard her mother thanking Mrs. Smiggins for the pumpkin pie. *Un-fucking-believable!*

"Dad." Dora called out to him.

He glanced up at her as he tied the ropes into a knot. "Yes."

"I want you to know something. Something I never thought I'd say to you."

He stepped off the pyre and nodded for her to continue. There was a look of benevolence in his expression. "Yes, my child."

"I'm never going to fucking forgive you for this." She snarled.

Her father's face became a mask of hatred. "You will still burn, witch."

Dora could smell wood burning as Principal Jackson lit a wooden torch near the entrance to the church. He held it aloft as he headed towards her, resembling a psychotic Olympic runner.

She searched the faces of the townspeople for someone who would come to her aid. Each face was watching with gleeful excitement, and not one contained an element of humanity in it. At that moment, they resembled the depictions of demons she had seen in her old grimoire. She decided all demon images must have been based on the faces of humanity because the actual demon in her closet never looked this evil. It was clear that this was what they wanted. No one was going to help her.

Frustration and anger burned through her veins as she struggled against the thick ropes, but they were rough and tightly bound her to the post. "Kieron," she cried. "Help me!"

Kieron was reading Dora's grimoire. He had found her summoning spell, but couldn't figure out why it had trapped him here. It was just a normal portal spell. He sighed and tried several different spells to try to open a portal back to Hell, but none of them worked.

There was a lot of noise coming from outside, but he ignored it, trying to concentrate on the spell. He frowned for a moment when he heard Dora calling his name. Panic caused a knot to tighten in his stomach, and his heart leapt into his throat. He dropped the book and rushed to the window, staring down in abject horror when he saw *his* Dora tied to a pyre by crazy people, who appeared to be about to light it.

Anger and fear burned through him. No, they would not harm his Dora-minx! He would save her from all of this. Hatred burned under his skin and something else shifted inside him. He realized he'd transformed into demon form when a guttural growl came from within his chest. He inhaled a deep breath to regain control of his temper and force his more appealing form to return.

He watched as Dora's father took hold of the fiery

torch, and he realized only a miracle could save her now.

He narrowed his eyes and clenched his hands into fists. With a grim smile, he called upon the forces of nature to bend them to his will.

A dark cloud amassed in the distance. It grew in size and traveled towards the church lawn. His eyes widened as the cloud drew closer, and he realized something had gone terribly wrong with his spell. That wasn't a cloud. *Oh shit!*

"Stop this! It's murder, you fucking idiot." Dora screamed at her father as he held up the burning torch. He shot her a cold glance and lit the pyre. The crowds around him cheered. Their chanting of 'burn the witch' grew in volume.

Dora kicked at the chips of wood under her feet, trying to push it away before licks of flames spread across the pyre towards her. She could smell the wood smoke, and the crowds had faded behind the growing flames.

"I hope you all die from grossly deforming genital warts!" she shouted when the heat of the fire warmed her skin. She was going to die. She was certain of it. Sweat beads popped up on her skin as the flames drew closer.

Dora closed her eyes in defeat, and fat tears streamed down her face. *I can't believe they're going to murder me.*

She frowned when a dark shadow passed over her closed eyelids. She heard an alien squawking fill the air, drowning out the baying crowd. She opened her eyes and peered up at the sky.

A black cloud filled with thousands of birds hovered over the front lawn. The noise coming from them was a deafening scream. Through the flames, she saw a blurry image of people staring up at the birds in horror. The birds emitted a loud squawk in unison before a white splat hit the pyre. Dora peered down at it. *Gross, bird shit.*

She glanced up again at the worst possible moment. An avalanche of bird shit fell from the skies and splattered all over the pyre and the people on the lawn. She blinked when she saw people knocked on their asses by the force of tons of bird excrement hitting them. A dirty snow-like liquid doused the flames in a loud splat, and the pyre became a white dripping mound.

Dora laughed when she saw the people of her town crying out in disgust, as they too became white bird-crap covered lumps. Some people threw up, others freaked out while trying to wipe off the ongoing rain of shit. She had to close her eyes as a mountain of bird excrement landed on her. *Eww!*

Eventually the rain of excrement ended, and the birds flew away with a squawk. The skies were no longer dark, and the fire was no longer burning.

Dora tested the ropes around her, but they still tightly bound her to the post. She shivered, feeling icky when she glanced down. She wrinkled up her nose. She was covered from head to toe in slimy bird shit. "Divine intervention," she muttered with a wry smile.

She gazed up towards her bedroom window at the

top of the church. Kieron was standing in it, waving with an apologetic smile on his face. He clicked his fingers, and the ropes binding her crumbled to dust. She rubbed her wrists before stepping off the pyre and walking down the lawn towards the church. People were wallowing in bird crap and crying at her feet. Some cowered as she walked past them, which made her grin.

She turned on her heel at the entrance of the church and faced them. "Now, you've incurred my wrath," she said in her darkest voice before turning around and walking back towards her room. *Time to get the fuck out of here.*

# HELL BOUND

D
ora dashed into her room. Her heart pounded, and she could barely breathe. She and Kieron had to leave here now before the morons downstairs scraped off the bird shit and decided to try burning her again. "Kieron, we need to—" She gasped for air as panic bubbled in her throat.

"Before you get angry." Kieron held up his hands in surrender. "I didn't mean to cover you in bird shi—"

"What? Oh, whatever, I'm alive, yay. We need to get the hell out of here, right now!" She swung her hand towards the door to point in the direction of danger. Some gloopy bird crap flew off her arm and splattered across Kieron's face. "They'll come back for me. We need to run!"

Kieron wiped his face with his sleeve, pulling a disgusted expression. "Don't you think you should clean yourself up first?"

"You're right! I'll be easy to spot like this." She struggled out of her T-shirt as quickly as possible.

"Wait," he said.

She glanced up to see an intense glint in his eyes. She paused pulling off her T-shirt, leaving it rucked up under her boobs and her midriff bare. "What?"

"I don't want the first time I see you naked to be when you're covered in bird shit," he said, his eyes glinting with a twinkle of mischief.

"Tough, we don't have much time." She snapped.

"So, you're saying at some point I get to see you naked?" He grinned.

Dora just scowled at him.

"Okay, we'll discuss that later, but I have a better idea for cleaning you up," he said. "And it's faster."

"What?"

"Magic." He winked and waved his hands over her body.

She watched the white liquid disappear from her clothes and skin as something cold washed over her. When the feeling faded, she glanced down to find herself thoroughly cleaned. "Ooh, that feels so weird." She tugged her T-shirt back down, and Kieron frowned. "What now?" she asked.

"It's okay. You can finish undressing before me now." He flashed a winning smile.

Dora kicked him in the shins. "We don't have time for this crap right now. Any minute those morons are going to rush in here and burn me alive. As soon as they realize it's just bird shit, they'll be storming up here. So please, can we get the hell out of here before that happens?"

"Of course, my minx. Where do you want to go?"

She hadn't thought that far ahead. She had no money and no car. Where did witches go for sanctuary? "Umm ... where do unburned witches go?"

Kieron appeared to ponder her question for a few seconds. "Well, burned ones go to Hell, but unburned ones. Hmm? I think some of them work for the IRS."

She sighed. "I'm beginning to wish we could go to Hell now."

"Why can't we?"

"You can't open a portal, remember."

"I can now. I figured it out when you were spending time with your witch burning family. When I summoned the rain and the birds came instead, it was obvious. Wait—does that mean you'll come to Hell with me, Dora-minx?"

"What was obvious?" She panicked when she heard people shouting outside. She ran to her bedroom door and locked it before pressing her ear against it and listening. She inhaled sharply. She could hear the sounds of stampeding feet rushing into the church.

"The magic here is backwards, hence shit instead of water. Instead of cleansing you I er, made you dirty. So to make a portal here, I just need to close a portal or use the spell to close one then one will open. It's just all backwards." He didn't appear concerned by the heavy footsteps pounding up the stairs.

"Kieron, we don't have much time," Dora cried as

fists hammered on the door. She heard a key going into the lock and pushed her body against the door before it could open. She braced herself on the flimsy wood as people far stronger than her pushed on the other side.

"Do you want me to take you to Hell, right now?" he asked.

"Yes!" she cried.

"What about your parents?"

"Fuck them!" she shouted as the door wedged open behind her. Her heart was hammering. If they caught her this time, they were going to do something worse than trying to burn her.

"I'm not fucking them, but I will take you away from here, fair Dora-minx." Kieron raised his hands into the air and muttered several words that she didn't recognize. A ball of colorful light swirled between his palms and hovered in the air by itself when he lowered his arms. Streaks of light shot off it as he stepped back towards her. It expanded and pulsed with electricity. Wind whipped around the room, swirling around the luminescent orb.

Something hard slammed into the door behind her, and she nearly lost her balance when the force of the blow shoved her forwards. She pressed back against the door, digging her heels into the carpet to keep it shut.

The orb grew into a large portal with spikes of electricity randomly shooting off it. A shiver of fear shot down her spine, but she ignored it. Her choices were limited. What was worse, a portal to Hell or being burned alive?

A warm hand curled around her fingers, and she

peered up into Kieron's blue eyes. They appeared so honest and full of warmth. Hell was better than this life—it just had to be.

"Come, Dora-minx. It is time to leave."

Dora tightly gripped his hand and followed him into the portal. She took one last look back at the world she was leaving behind. Her bedroom door burst open a few seconds after she left it. Several people tumbled through the doorway and landed face first on her carpet. She frowned when she saw her parents standing numbly in the doorway with a large group of angry townspeople crowding around them. They all froze with shock on their faces as they stared at the portal. *Goodbye, motherfuc—*

In a blast of fiery red light, they were gone. All she could see were flashes of lava lights speeding past her eyes. Kieron's hand gripped hers. Her body felt compacted as if being pulled through the eye of a needle. She screamed, closing her eyes and hoping it would be over soon. It all stopped when she landed on hard gravel with a thud.

She warily opened one eye. She could still feel Kieron holding her hand, and she glanced in his direction to find him lying beside her. He had also landed face first on the deserted highway. She released his hand before rolling over and groaning. She gingerly checked nothing was broken before reaching over to him. She brushed his broad shoulder. "Kieron, are you okay?"

"Ohh, I hate that bit." He rolled over and sat up. "I'm fine. Are you okay?" He leaned towards her and brushed some gravel out of her hair.

"I think so. Where are we?"

"The Highway to Hell." He smiled. "You're safe now."

# 10

## HIGHWAY TO HELL

D ora stared down the endless highway. The sky glowed red and pink through the dark gray clouds. Dusty wastelands flanked both sides of the road in desolate miles of red sand dunes dotted with spiky plants and a few skeletal Joshua trees, which were black silhouettes across the flat landscape. In the distance, flaming volcanoes sat upon the horizon.

She got to her feet and turned around. The road appeared to be the same in the opposite direction, a duplicate reflection in every way. "Which way to do we go?"

"It doesn't matter," Kieron replied.

"Huh?" She wondered if she looked as dumb as she felt right now.

"It all leads to the same place."

"So which way do we walk?"

"On this road, you don't walk." He stood up and guided her to the side of the road. "You hitch a ride."

"How?"

"By hitchhiking," he replied.

"Isn't that er, dangerous?"

He laughed and shook his head. "You humans are so weird. You'll risk your life on what you digest, but you're scared of hitchhiking."

"Well that's when you're most likely to meet a psychopath." She attempted to explain.

Kieron laughed again. "Psychopaths have their own bars in Hell. They don't waste time on empty highways. You'll see."

She shivered and wondered what she was getting herself into. This probably wasn't the best idea she'd ever had. "Is it okay that I'm here?" she asked.

"What, in Hell?"

"Yeah, like, am I allowed to be here?"

"It's a gray area, but don't worry. I'm sure my dad can sort out clearance for you. And, Dora-minx …" He clicked his fingers, and a jacket appeared in his hands. He helped her put it on and wrapped it around her shoulders. "I won't let anything bad happen to you."

Dora studied his face. His eyes were the clearest blue, and she loved looking into them. There was something comforting about how clear and honest they were. There was something comforting about him. "Thank you, Kieron," she said, flashing a smile.

"You're welcome. Now, let's get a ride." He winked and held out his thumb over the empty highway.

From out of nowhere, a massive black rig roared down the road towards them. Evil red headlights glowed like eyes in the darkness as it loomed menacingly towards them. It came to a screeching halt beside them with the engine growling and smoke puffing out of the big grill at the front of it.

The passenger door swung open to reveal a grizzly truck driver leering down at them. The driver was massive. He had a few days growth of stubble on his jaw and a lit cigar hanging from his lips. He grinned down at them, holding the cigar in his teeth. "Hop in kiddies."

Dora really didn't want to get into the cab of the truck. She glanced at Kieron for assistance, but he was already climbing into the rig.

She reluctantly shrank away from the truck as the driver watched her, grinning. After a moment of being under his scrutiny, she noticed his smile slip. "Eww! No way," he squealed like a girl.

"Huh?" She frowned and forgot her fears in an instant.

"Aww come on, man! Don't be like that," Kieron said.

"I may not be a demon of many rules, but I do have some standards," the driver said.

Dora was beginning to feel like a leper.

"She's okay," Kieron protested.

"She'll stink up my truck!" the driver snapped.

She glared at the driver and put her hands on her hips. "What did you just say?"

"Sugar, that stinky soul of yours needs darkening up before you get into my truck."

Kieron rolled his eyes. "Fucking soulists!"

"Dude, your truck already stinks of rotten farts," she replied. "I can't make it smell any worse!"

"You try carrying sprouts across Hell and back on a daily basis, and see how rotten you smell." The truck driver defended his rig.

"Why sprouts?" she asked.

"About fifty per cent of humans hate sprouts, even evil the ones." Kieron answered. "They make a great torture device."

"That's what this big evil-looking truck does? It ships fucking vegetables, and *I'm* the one with a stinky white soul here. Move over, man. I'm getting in your damn truck." Dora shook her head and climbed up in to the cab of the rig, loudly slamming the door shut behind her.

"I sometimes ship lost souls too," the truck driver muttered.

"Come on, sprout man. Stop whining and put some pedal to the metal." Dora commanded.

The driver snarled, and the truck's engine roared into life.

Kieron chuckled. "That's my girl."

"I am not your girl." She snapped. "I am *a* girl."

"I dunno." Kieron shrugged. "You are moving in with me. That's almost dating."

The truck driver snorted.

"What?" Kieron asked.

"I thought that when my girlfriend moved in. She turned out to be a bloody banshee. Trust me son, keep your own space."

Kieron appeared to consider it for a moment. "I may

not be as old as you, but I'm pretty certain having a girl sleeping in my bed is a good thing. Did you try gagging your banshee?"

Dora punched Kieron in the arm several times.

"Ow, ow, what the hell? Owww!" He tried to duck the punches, but since he was squashed between Dora and the driver, he had nowhere to go.

"That is why you can't gag them." The truck driver commented as Dora pounded on Kieron until he begged her to stop.

"Dora-minx, why are you attacking me?" he cried.

"Gag *them*, are you shitting me?" She smacked him a few more times to make her point.

"I didn't mean *you*! Seriously, when you meet a Banshee, you'll understand."

"I doubt I will."

"No really, there is a difference. I'd never gag a succubus unless they liked it."

The truck driver belched out a dirty chuckle. Dora flicked Kieron on the end of the nose. "Gawd, are all demons perverts?"

The truck driver wiggled his eyebrows at her, making her involuntarily shrink back against the door of the truck. His creepiness was freaking her out.

She glanced at Kieron when she heard him growl possessively, but found herself staring at the back of his head as he turned to face the driver. "Dora is under my protection." Kieron's voice was cold and deeper than usual. It was guttural sounding and ominous.

"Hey, no worries, man." The truck driver paled and

widened his eyes in fear. "I'm not into girls with souls anyway."

Dora stared at the back of Kieron's head. His blond hair was the same, but his shirt had tightened over his muscled back and shoulders. *Did he just grow in size?* She blinked and watched his shoulders sink as he slowly exhaled. "Kieron?"

He turned to face her. For a second, she could have sworn his blue eyes were glowing red, and horns poked out of his forehead. The moment passed quickly then his eyes were clear blue again. She frowned at him and pressed herself against the door of the truck. Something weird was happening.

"It's okay, Dora-minx." He took her hand and squeezed it. "Don't be scared. I'd never hurt you."

"Yeah? That helps. What just happened to your eyes?"

"Um, I don't know. I can't see my own eyes."

She felt suspicious of him for the first time. "There's something you're not telling me."

"There are many things I haven't told you." He smiled.

"Like what?"

"My favorite color is blue. I like peanuts in my cheese sandwich. Oh, and I like fluffy kittens."

"To eat?" the driver asked.

Kieron gasped, appearing appalled by the suggestion. "No! Why would you eat a kitten?"

"Oh crap, you're one of those *vegetarians* aren't you?" The truck driver spat out the words in disgust. "I should have known!"

"Do not anger me again, driver."

"I have a name you know." The driver snapped.

"What is it?" Dora asked.

"That's it! Out of my truck, now!" The driver slammed on the breaks. Both Dora and Kieron jerked forward in their seats as the passenger door swung open all by itself.

"What did I do?" Dora asked.

"Out!" the driver snarled.

Kieron nodded at Dora and gestured for her climb out. She pushed herself out of the rig and jumped onto the highway. She heard Kieron land on the road behind her. Once they were both standing at the roadside, she turned to face the driver. "Seriously what did I do?"

The door slammed shut in her face, and the rig zoomed past them and down the highway. She turned to face Kieron. "What?"

He shook his head. "You never ask a demon their name. You should know that."

"Why not?"

"Because you can use it to control them."

"But I know your name."

He coughed and peered at his feet. "That's a ... er, a personal preference."

Dora frowned at him. "What does that mean?"

"I'll tell you when you're older," he said. "Now, follow me. Let's go home."

"Don't we need to hitch another ride?"

"No, it's just over there." He pointed to a vast castle

on a hill at the side of the highway. Haunting black spires pointed sharply into the sky from the numerous turrets of the massive building. The onyx structure had carvings of demons littering every ledge. Fire shot out of several windows in short, sharp blasts. The entrance was the open mouth of a demonic creature with sharp teeth glinting above the large wooden doors.

"Home sweet home," he said in a cheerful voice.

"Oh shit," Dora replied.

# CASTLE LASCHER

**D**ora peered up at the sharp teeth surrounding the doorframe. They glinted with a reddish hue from the firelight reflected in them. "So this is your house?" she asked, glancing at Kieron as he unlocked the door.

"Yes, and hopefully no one's home," he replied as he pushed open the double doors and invited her to enter the massive castle.

She took an apprehensive step across the threshold. She didn't know what Kieron's parents were like. *What if they don't like me? Parents never like me.* She stepped onto the marble tiles and entered the castle with a bubble of panic growing in her stomach.

She surveyed the interior of the opulent gothic castle. There was a large foyer with a high ceiling. The centerpiece was a sweeping staircase adorned with a thick red carpet. She ran her fingers over the red and gold wallpaper decorating the wall behind her. It was furry to touch. The castle was majestic and bizarre with an array of red, black, white or gold ornaments decorating it.

She jumped when Kieron touched her arm. "Come on," he said. "Let's get to my room before my paren—"

"YOU DARE TO SHOW YOUR FACE HERE?" A voice thundered through the castle. The deep, dark growl sounded to Dora as if Satan himself had spoken. She gripped Kieron's hand as her heart leapt into her throat. *Oh shit, oh shit, oh shit …*

"Aww crap," Kieron said with a sigh.

Dora's eyes widened when an enormous black demon flew into the room. Its body bulged with veiny muscles. It flexed its long fingers and toes. Sharp talons sprang out of them as it hovered in the air over her and Kieron. Its scaly wings spanned the width of the room, sending hot air rushing into her face with every flap and causing her dark hair to blow around her. She stared up at the face of the demon. Its eyes glowed blood-red, and sharp fangs poked out of its mouth over its bottom lip.

"Dad, what the fuck?" Kieron cried. "Are you trying to embarrass me?"

Dora gulped. *That thing is Kieron's father?*

"YOU'LL SUFFER A WORLD OF TORMENT FOR YOUR ACTIONS." The demon bellowed as it landed on the floor in front of her and Kieron. "And you've really upset your mother," it added.

"I didn't do anything wrong." Kieron protested. "Dad, could you at least look more reasonable. We have a guest."

"Fine," the demon muttered. "But don't think

having a house guest will save you."

Dora watched with awe as the demon shrank in size, and its skin became pale. It changed into a middle-aged man with slicked-back black hair and dark blue eyes. He wore a black suit and was attractive for an older man.

"Your mother has been flaying anything that moves since you missed her family barbeque." Kieron's father told him in a crisp and pleasant voice. "Now, who do we have here?"

A nervous blush warmed Dora's skin as the man studied every inch of her with his eyes.

"This is Dora. I just saved her from a crazy holy man and invited her to live with us. So she's moving in." Kieron rushed his words, gripping her elbow and guiding her towards the staircase.

"Hold on there, sport, not so fast. Young lady, Dora is it? Come here please." Kieron's father beckoned her over with an elegant wave of his hand.

She heard Kieron groan as she walked over to his father and looked him straight in the eye. *This is gonna suck.*

He held out his hand to greet her. "I'm Lord Lascher. It's nice to meet you, Dora. You may call me Lionel."

She glanced back at Kieron, who nervously shifted from one foot to the other while staring at them. Turning towards Lord Lasher, she took his offered hand and shook it, flashing what she hoped was a polite smile. "It's um, nice to meet you too, Lord L—er, Lionel."

"What brings you to Hell Dora, aside from my imbecile of a son?"

She heard Kieron groan again behind her, and she fought to conceal a grin. "I er, was being burned as a witch, and Hell sounded like a pleasant alternative. Kieron kindly offered his hospitality. I hope it's not an inconvenience?"

"No, no, not at all, we have lots of room at Castle Lascher. It'll be a pleasure getting acquainted with you, I'm sure." Lionel's pleasant smile helped abate any remaining anxiousness she was feeling. "So tell me Dora, did you burn as a witch and meet Kieron when you first arrived here?"

"Um, no, Ki—"

"Dad, come on! What's with the Spanish Inquisition?" Kieron interrupted.

"I'm just making polite enquiries," Lionel protested. "You were saying, my dear?" Lionel turned back to her with an inquisitive glitter in his dark eyes.

"Um …" She glanced at Kieron, who was shaking his head in an urgent manner. "No, I didn't burn," she said, trying to understand what Kieron wanted her to do.

"Ah, how did you die if you don't mind me asking?" Lionel enquired.

"Um … I er, didn't." She saw Kieron slap himself in the forehead.

Lionel narrowed his dark eyes at Kieron before turning back to her. "I see."

"Dad—" Kieron began.

"Don't you Dad me, you little sod. Your mother is going to kill you *again* for this!" Lionel snapped at him.

"It's not that big a deal!" Kieron shouted at his father.

"Not that big a deal? You've brought home a human—a live one!"

"She's not like the other ones. She understands evil, and she's a witch."

Lionel shook his head and shot Dora a sideways glance. "Young demons, always thinking with their horns," he sounded apologetic. "And you!" Lionel pointed to Kieron. "You're lucky your mother is flaying in the kitchen right now, or I'd be scraping you off the walls."

"What, er … Is there a problem with me being a human?" she asked.

"The thing is, Dora. Humans don't come to Hell alive because we have a quota to meet. We create demons out of souls. If your soul hasn't been condemned to Hell, we can't do much with it. Souls are kept inside vaults in Hell, not inside soft little humans. It upsets the natural order of things around here when a living human drops by," Lionel said, offering her a sympathetic smile.

"So, I can't stay in Hell?" she asked.

"Not with a clean soul inside you, no."

"And who decides that?" She got annoyed. Even Hell didn't want her.

"Well the panel at Judgment Day makes the final decision." Lionel frowned before examining her as if she was an interesting science experiment.

"So who do I have to kill to change their minds?"

Lionel laughed. "I like your way of thinking. Maybe there is hope for you after all."

"She can take the test with me. Come on, it'll be

fun," Kieron suggested to his father with a hopeful expression on his face.

"Do you think you've got what it takes to beat the darkest demons in Hell at being truly evil?" Lionel asked Dora.

"Can I cheat?" she asked. She was tired of being the outcast, and she was certain she had enough pent up anger to do some damage.

Lionel laughed again. "A good answer, fair Dora, you shall have your chance at staying in Hell. But ..." He shifted his eyes towards Kieron. "We do not tell Lady Lascher about this. Do you understand?"

"Yes, Dad." Kieron nodded.

"Not a problem." Dora agreed.

"Good, now both of you, go to Kieron's room. I need to break it to Lady Lascher that we have a guest for dinner."

They turned and walked towards the staircase.

"Oh, and Dora," Lionel called.

She turned and held her breath. *What now?*

"Do try to break some rules before dinner. It'll darken that soul up a bit," Lionel said with a wink.

She grinned. Finally, something she would enjoy.

Dora paced the room to try to walk off some of the nervous energy knotting up her insides. She heard a deep sigh and glanced back at Kieron who was sitting on his bed and staring at his feet. "What's wrong?" She spun on her heel to face him.

"I am worried. It is harder to keep you safe here than I thought it would be." He stood up and walked over to her.

She backed away from him on instinct, which was confusing even to her. Now that she was in Hell and had seen a demon, she didn't feel comfortable with Kieron.

She studied him from a safe distance. He looked the same. His golden hair curled around the collar of his white shirt, which was now crumpled and grimy. His big blue eyes still shone with innocence. Well, right now they shone with surprise, but they were the same.

Something was wrong though. The questions filling her mind altered her impression of Kieron. The most frightening question remained unanswered. What was he underneath his handsome exterior? *A black scaly thing if his father is anything to go by.* "When was the last time you changed your clothes?" She attempted to cover up her reluctance to be near him.

His face flushed with embarrassment. "I-I—we were stuck on Earth, and you didn't like it when I stole things. What was I supposed to do?"

"Well, we're not stuck on Earth now." She pointed out. "Get chang—."

"GYARRRRRRHG!" A female shriek echoed through the castle. Dora spun around to face the closed bedroom door. Her heart raced as she stared at the shaking wooden frame. Lights sparked under the door, and the wood panels bubbled out as if there was a lot of pressure behind them. The door continued to expand, stretching out into an impossible curve as pressure on the other side of it pushed against the wood.

A loud bang made her jump backwards in pure terror. She landed against a wall of muscle and shivered when strong arms encircled her waist. *Kieron?* It took her a long time to glance down at the arms around her waist. *Will they be human?*

She sighed with relief when she peered down to see human-looking tanned arms around her. They were lightly muscled and adorned with a smattering of golden hairs. Her pulse raced when his hot breath grazed her cheek. She realized he was shirtless behind her.

"W-wha—what are you doing?" Her heart pounded for more than one reason now. The door expanded towards them with green and gold lights shooting out from under it. Meanwhile, Kieron stood half-naked behind her, which was doing all kinds of insane things to her insides.

"What you asked of me, Dora-minx. I was getting changed." His voice was close to her ear. It was soft and tantalizing. She forgot about the things on the other side of the door and inhaled a slow deep breath. She turned in Kieron's arms and faced him. They stared at each other for a long moment of silence. Their heavy breathing was the only sound she could hear. He was going to kiss her, she was sure of it. She wanted him to. *What the Hell, right? If I'm going to lose my soul anyway why not enjoy myself for once?*

A loud crash behind them broke the spell as the door exploded. She snapped out of her daze and looked over her shoulder towards the doorway. Green smoke filled the opening, and a silhouette of a woman holding a blade and some kind of slab appeared in mist.

Dora gulped as the shadow walked towards them. Her hands trembled against Kieron's naked chest from fear and panic until the figure stepped through the haze. Dora frowned when a petit brunette wearing a sixties style dress and an apron stepped out of the smoke. She carried a chocolate fudge cake and a cake slice. "Kieron Lascher, you put a shirt on this minute!" The woman snapped at him.

Kieron groaned as he released Dora. "Yes, mother."

Dora shivered as his warm hands brushed over her waist before leaving her.

"Dora dear, it's so nice to meet you. Can I tempt you?" She offered her a piece of cake.

Dora decided it was wiser to accept the cake rather than to point out that Kieron was far more tempting right now. "It's nice to meet you too, Lady Lascher," she mumbled, helping herself to a piece of cake.

"Kieron's such an awful host. Why, you must be exhausted, you poor thing. Come with me, and we'll get you settled in your own room, shall we?" A sparkle of something insane glittered in Lady Lascher's eyes. She was small and unassuming, prim and proper in every way, but she caused a shiver of fear to run down Dora's spine when she looked at her.

"S-su-sure," Dora stammered as she peeked back at Kieron for assistance, but he was shrugging into a clean shirt with a look of helplessness on his face.

She didn't know what to do, so she followed Lady
Lascher out of the room and into the dark winding
corridors of Castle Lascher.

## DEMON IN LAW

"You have a lovely castle Lady Lascher." Dora couldn't shake the nervous feeling as she followed the silent Lady Lascher down the long corridors of the castle. The walls were black glass, lit only by burning torches dotted randomly down the hallway.

"Thank you." Lady Lascher turned back and flashed a brief smile at her, but the smile never reached her eyes. "All my friends call me Anika."

Dora smiled back before averting her eyes. The woman gave her the creeps. She tried to shake off the feeling and peered at her reflection in the corridor walls instead. She was still wearing the same T-shirt and mini skirt from yesterday. *I need to buy some new clothes or something.*

"Anika, do you know where I can get some clothes?" she asked as they came to the end of the corridor. They turned and headed down a narrow stone staircase, which appeared endless.

Anika remained silent as they walked down the stone stairs to what appeared to be a basement. She turned and studied Dora when they left the stairs and headed down a corridor in the basement. "I said my friends may call me Anika." Her voice was cold, and her eyes glowed red for a second before her plastic smile resumed its place on her lips.

*Oh fuck,* Dora thought.

"Come. Let me show you to your room," Anika said as she led Dora down the stone corridor and past several dungeons. She stopped outside a cell and opened the door before gesturing for her to enter it. "You'll learn to summon clothing soon enough. Now that you're dead, you'll find you are capable of much more than the living."

Dora peered into the dungeon. It was a bare stone room with shackles on the walls and bars on the window. *Oh, double fuck!*

She realized she was screwed. Lady Lascher was supposed to think she was a dead soul, but she was still alive and didn't have any powers. *I don't have access to a bathroom either, by the looks of it,* she thought, peering around the room. "Um, not to sound ungrateful, but where do I sleep?" She stepped into the cell and eyed the hard stone floor.

She heard the door slam shut behind her and the grinding thunk of a lock falling into place. She spun around to see Lady Lascher's evil smile through the bars of the cell. "On the floor until you learn to be a decent demon," she hissed.

Dora narrowed her eyes. "Are you fucking shitting

me?"

A force slammed into Dora and pinned her against the back wall. She could feel a hand gripping her throat and holding her up against the stone, but when she peered down there was nothing there. She glared at Anika, who offered her a polite smile while watching her through the bars.

Burning hot breath warmed her cheek as a dark voice growled in her ear. "If you think you're good enough for my son, you're sadly mistaken, bitch!"

"What?" She gasped.

"I said," Anika replied in a polite tone through the bars of the cell. "You'll have to join us for the family barbeque tomorrow." Her voice was light and pleasant, nothing like the voice in Dora's ear.

"Do I have to stay here until then?" Dora asked as she tried to pull the invisible hand away from her throat.

"If you try to leave, I'll rip out your entrails and paint the room red with them." The dark voice growled into her ear.

"Get some rest, dear. You'll feel better in the morning for it." Anika smiled before walking away. As she disappeared from view, the force pinning Dora to the wall went with her.

Dora rubbed her neck and coughed. *Does she have a split personality or something?* She scowled and tried the door, but it wouldn't budge.

She explored the room, trying to find a way to break out of the dungeon. *Screw the demon-in-law from Hell and my entrails. I always wanted a red room, anyway,* she thought as she rattled the bars of the cell, attempting to break open the door.

Kieron paced his room with a knot of anxiety tightening in his stomach. *Where did she take Dora?* He knew his mother all too well and feared what she had done to Dora. His mother was unreasonable at the best of times.

The loud gong announcing dinner chimed, interrupting his pacing.

He flung open his door and raced down the sweeping staircase towards the immense dining room, hoping to find Dora waiting for him there.

He came to an abrupt halt when he reached the end of the long ebony dining table. He frantically scanned the room. *Where is she?* The knot tightened in his stomach when he realized the only occupants of the room appeared to be his mother and father. While seated at the far end of the table, his parents turned to stare at him with curious expressions.

"Where's Dora?" Kieron gasped.

His father shrugged, and his mother composed an innocent expression. "Who?"

"Where is she?" He slammed his fists onto the table in anger and fear.

"Sit down and eat your dinner. If you mean the new demon, she's resting in her room," his mother said.

"Has she eaten anything?" Kieron asked.

"She's a new demon. She won't be hungry for days."

His mother waved away his question. "Now sit!"

He panicked. She wasn't a new demon, but he couldn't tell his mother that.

"Which wing did you put her in?" Kieron's father spoke up.

"The southern one," his mother replied.

"Where we put the tortured souls?" Kieron exploded. His heart pounded with fear. What kind of torture was poor Dora going through in there?

"It's not the best guest room to choose," Kieron's father said.

"It's airy, and she'll meet other souls there. I thought it'd help her adjust—Kieron if you don't sit down and eat your dinner, I'm going to get angry." His mother snapped.

He was furious, but he knew better than to cross his mother. He threw himself into the chair and began eating his dinner as fast as possible. He needed to get to Dora before something awful happened to her—the tortured souls were lunatics. If she were stuck in a dungeon, she wouldn't be able to escape the crazy spirits who haunted that wing. He shot a helpless look at his father while shoveling a forkful of vegetables into his mouth.

His father frowned back at him and gave him a subtle nod. "Dora's past the adjusting stage, my love. I think she'll do much better in Kieron's wing. After all, she is here to help him study for his exams." Kieron's father was a convincing liar.

"I thought she was a new demon. How can she help Kieron?" his mother asked.

"She was exceptionally evil when she as alive, my dear. I think she could best some of the teachers at the academy. You really do need to give her the chance to show you what she can do." His father brushed his lips with a napkin and stood up.

His mother sighed. "If you think she has it in her, then okay, but I won't have her running around the castle acting like a human. Keep her out of my way until she's ready."

Kieron devoured the plate of food in front of him before jumping up from the table. "May I be excused?"

"Yes, fine. Go and move her to your wing." His mother waved him away.

"I'll go with him and ensure it's done without any disruption, dear," his father said.

Kieron followed his father out of the dining room at a steady pace, fighting against the urge to run to the south wing to reach Dora sooner.

As soon as they were out of sight of his mother, Kieron and his father glanced at each other. "Shit!" they said in unison before racing towards the southern wing.

"Nooooo!" Kieron heard Dora's cry followed by an animalistic shriek. He dashed down the corridor towards the dungeon. *What are they doing to her? No, no, no. I'm coming, Dora-minx. I'll save you!*

He came to an abrupt halt at her cell door, panting for air. When he glanced into the cell, he frowned and blinked at the scene before him. After a few seconds, his father caught up with him. They stared in silence through the bars at Dora.

"You idiot," Dora said to a tortured soul sitting opposite her. "You can't bluff with four kings." She gestured to the three other tortured souls in the room. "Seriously guys, none of you have played poker before? How is that even possible?"

The tortured souls around her shrugged. A large one with green goo dripping from his eyes chuckled before letting out an insane shriek. A big blob of goo splattered on the floor in front of him.

"Dude, you're so cleaning that up. No way I'm taking the blame from Lady Lamer for it." She told the soul, who grumbled something unintelligible in reply.

Kieron stared at Dora in awe. She'd not only tamed the tortured souls, but was also playing poker with them! "Dora, are you okay?" he asked through the bars.

She turned to face him. He sighed with relief when he saw her bright smile lighting up her face. "Kieron these guys are fab. Did you know Larry could fart fire? It's fuckin' epic!" She gestured to the skinny soul sitting across from her who demonstrated by shooting a blast of fire out of his backside.

"No, I did not know that. Um, I came here to save … er, to take you to nicer rooms." He didn't know what to say. No one had ever tamed a tortured soul this fast before.

"Impressive," Kieron's dad said behind him. He glanced back to see his father was watching Dora with a gleam in his eyes. Kieron didn't like the gleam, at all.

"Oh, hi Lionel." She waved at him.

Kieron waited for his father to unlock the cell before he rushed into the room. He needed to make sure she was okay. He offered her a hand, and she accepted by placing her small hand into his. He pulled her up from the floor, keeping hold of her hand once he had it in his grasp. She was far too carefree. In Hell, other demons would take advantage of that kind of thing.

A glow of warm happiness flowed through him when she gave him a brief hug. His pulse raced until she released him and turned to face the tortured souls.

"It's been a total blast guys. Once I'm settled in my new room, I'll come back and we can play again, okay?"

The tortured souls nodded and made agreeable noises. "Poker night." Larry suggested.

"That's a fab idea," she replied. "Friday night is now poker night."

The souls all nodded in agreement before evaporating from the room, leaving tendrils of smoke in their wake.

"Come on. Let's get you to a better room." Kieron tugged on her hand to guide her out of the cell. He was relieved when she followed him.

"Yeah, one with a bathroom would be good," she said with a laugh.

Kieron hugged her. He couldn't help it. He'd been so worried about her and was overjoyed she was okay.

"Um Kieron, does your mom have a multiple personality disorder? Is she bipolar or something?" Dora peered up at him with concern in her eyes.

He heard his dad laughing behind them. "That's my girl. Wait until you meet the rest of the family, Dora. You'll love the barbeque."

Kieron groaned. He hoped his grandmother wasn't coming to the family barbeque this week. She was a nightmare.

# 13

## THROW ANOTHER SHRIMP ON THE BARBIE

Dora smoothed down the knee-length black dress she wore. It was silky and strapless with a fitted bodice and a flared skirt. Kieron had conjured it for her, along with a pair of black sandals and diamond earrings.

She looked in the mirror and twirled, grinning. *Good taste in clothes, and apparently he can dance too. I'd swear he was gay if I didn't know better.*

She was in her new room at Castle Lascher. The room was stylishly decorated and had a big, comfortable bed in it. She'd been overjoyed when she discovered it also had a private bathroom with a luxurious tub and a power shower.

She felt much better for having a bath and putting on clean clothes. Better, but not perfect. Tonight was the family barbecue. She didn't know what to expect because everything in Hell was so weird. She had a feeling Castle Lascher was weirder than most places in Hell.

A gentle knock at the door startled her. *Oh no, he's here already! I must be crazy to willingly meet more of Kieron's family.* She shook her head and tried to shake off a feeling of impending doom as she walked over to the door and opened it.

Kieron stood in the doorway, wearing an old-fashioned black suit that fit nicely across his broad shoulders and accentuated his lean form. He flashed a smile that lit up his face, adding a bright sparkle to his eyes. Something fluttered in her chest. *Okay, that's not fair. He looks hotter than I do!*

He held out his arm for her. "M'lady." He winked.

She took his arm and peered up at him. "I ain't no lady." She grinned.

His eyes widened with a look of shock before he laughed. "Silly, Dora-minx, you're a lady here."

"Huh?" She frowned. *What the hell does that mean?*

"Lady Dora-minx," he said. "Dad registered you last night."

"Registered me where, exactly?"

"At the Demon Academy ... er, school to you."

"I have to go to school?" She scowled. That sounded like work.

"It's okay. We're going together. You'll be fine."

Panic bubbled in her stomach. She didn't do well in school. She never had. Schools tended to have one substantial flaw—people went to them. She could handle most things, but other people were just impossible. School grouped people together and made them worse. It forced them to gather and compete for popularity, grades or some other stupid crap. It didn't matter what they competed for, they still turned into total assholes. "Do I really have to go to school?"

"It's the only way you can stay here. You have to pass the Judgment Day tests."

"Ugh! Can't I just read evil in a book?"

"Um, no, evil is more practical here, less reading and more action."

"Okay, I'll go, but I won't like it," she replied with a feeling of defeat.

"Don't worry about it tonight. You have enough to worry about—like surviving my relatives." Kieron frowned.

"Are they that bad?"

"Let's just say, my mother is a dream in comparison to them."

Dora gulped. *Is it even possible for there to be anyone worse than Lady Lascher?* She glanced up and realized Kieron was staring at her.

"What?"

"Oh, nothing." He turned away as his face flushed with color.

"What?" she repeated and elbowed him in the side, so he'd look in her direction, again.

"It's just y-y-you look very pretty in your dress," he stammered.

"*That* has you blushing?"

"Well, no ... sort of." He coughed, clearly embarrassed. "I was wondering what you looked like under the dress."

She pushed him over. "You're like a walking hormone!" she said with disgust.

He looked up at her from the floor with surprise on his face. "I don't know why you did that?"

"I did it so you would stop imagining what was under my dress." She snapped.

"Well I don't have to imagine it now. I can see it at this angle," he replied as he tilted his head sideways.

Dora yelped and jumped away from him, hugging her skirt around her legs. *Okay, he's obviously not gay.*

"Hurry up you two. If you're late, I won't be responsible for what happens to you." Lionel's voice bellowed up the stairs.

Kieron got up off the floor and brushed down his suit. "Sorry, sometimes I get the devil in me." He held out his hand to her.

She wondered if he meant that literally as she took his hand and followed him down the stairs. They crossed the foyer and walked down a wide corridor into a vast ballroom filled with demons.

The room had tall onyx pillars dotted around the edges of the bustling dance floor. Vast buffet tables brimming with food and drinks ran along both sides of the room.

Dora stared at the guests in awe. Massive beasts with horns and fangs mingled with sexy succubae. People in all styles of dress, from extravagant costumes to dull beige suits, chatted easily with demonic imps and ghostly apparitions.

A giant octopus-looking creature with eight slimy

tentacles coming out of its back roared and wrapped its arms around an unassuming man in a frightening hug.

"Dora, stop staring," Kieron whispered out of the side of his mouth.

"What is it?" she whispered back.

"Uncle Bernard." He shifted his eyes to the octopus man.

She attempted to avert her eyes to the ceiling and not stare, but a green dragon flew into her line of sight and shot flames from its massive jaws onto a huge fire pit at the end of the room. The flames burned brightly, and all the guests turned to applaud. "Holy fucking crap," she whispered to Kieron.

"Don't swear here," he hissed back.

"Sorry, holy crap." She amended her words.

He turned to stare at her. "Dora, *fucking* is okay here, but *holy* is a swear word. Oh hell …" He shook his head and let out a worried sigh. "There are so many things you can do wrong here."

She shivered. "I'll be okay though, right?"

His expression did not make her feel terribly confident. "Yeah …" He surveyed the room and winced. "It'll be fine, just—try not to speak."

"Okay. Don't worry. I can do this," she  said with more confidence than she felt.

"Is that my grandbaby, all grown up and with a girl? He's not gay after all." A female voice shrieked.

"Oh crap," Kieron muttered.

Dora spun around to face the direction of the voice and saw what appeared to be a ten-foot Barbie doll walking towards them. *Well, if there is such a thing as 'BDSM Barbie'*, she thought.

"*That's* your grandmother?" She gaped, pointing to the giant blond amazon. She was wearing red leather underwear and dragging a short man behind her on a dog leash. She looked about twenty-five years old and sultry with curves in all the right places, but she was massive and towered over most of the people in the room.

As she made a beeline for them, Dora raised herself to her full height of five-foot eight, but it was still too short to do anything other than look up at BDSM Barbie.

"Hey Grandma." Kieron sounded reluctant as he greeted the vivacious blonde.

"That's all I get?" the amazon shouted. "Come 'ere, you little midget of cuteness, and give Grammy a hug." She scooped Kieron into her arms and almost suffocated him with her massive bosom. "Oh, eww!" His muffled cries came from somewhere between the fleshy mounds.

Dora bit the inside of her cheek to stop herself from bursting out laughing.

"Shrimp, Shrimp, Shrimp!" She heard chanting and glanced towards the back of the room to see crowds of demons gathering around the fire pit.

"Ah, ha!" Kieron's Grammy released him and raised her fist in the air. "Let's throw another shrimp on the barbie!" she cried.

Dora glanced at Kieron. *What the hell does that mean?*

He shook his head. "She's from down under," he muttered in explanation.

"What Australia?" Dora asked.

"No, down under Hell; beneath the lava lakes. It's the level of Hell that doesn't get into the history books."

"Why not?"

"Because it's full of sexual deviants," he muttered.

"Shrimp, shrimp, shrimp!" the crowds roared. The man on the leash behind Kieron's grandmother sighed. He was about five-feet tall and slightly balding. He was wearing black leather pants and a dog collar. "I'm not doing it!" He snapped.

At that moment, a three-foot-tall blue demon with long ears and fuzzy orange hair scurried past them, hurriedly making its way to the exit.

"Ooh, a mini shrimp." Kieron's grandmother scooped it up in her arms and carried it through the crowds over her head. It wriggled and screamed. The crowds cheered as she launched the little demon into the fire pit.

"It'll take weeks for its hair to grow back." The man on the leash commented as he picked up his own leash and twirled the end of it.

"Dora, meet my grandfather, Hickory Lascher," Kieron introduced the man on a leash as demons cheered at the blazing fire pit, and the blue creature's screams echoed through the room.

# 14
## BATTLE OF THE BITCHES

"It's a pleasure to meet you." Dora held out her dainty hand to Kieron's grandfather.

Kieron noticed surprise flash across Hickory's expression before he gathered his wits and shook her hand. "It's a pleasure to meet you too, Dora. I hear you'll be joining us at the Daemon Academia?"

"Y-yes, I think I am," she stammered.

Kieron sensed by her expression that she was wondering how old students were at the academy. He knew her well enough to realize that the idea of endless school was her own personal Hell. "Grandpa is the Headmaster." He told Dora with a smile. A warm glow of happiness spread through his body when she breathed a sigh of relief and smiled back.

"So you're the principal?" Dora asked Hickory.

"Headmaster," Hickory said. He growled like a dog. "Principals in Hell suffer. They do not teach."

"Oh, Sorry," she apologized.

Kieron groaned on the inside. She was going to have to learn Hell-speak faster.

"Well, well, well. If it isn't my favorite new girl." Kieron heard his dad's voice interrupt when he wandered over with Lady Lascher. He greeted his father with a nod because he'd saved Dora from asking more stupid questions, but he didn't like the 'my girl' reference. In fact, it made him wary of his father's interest in her. *She's my Dora-minx, not his!*

"Deviant devils!" His mother swore, her eyes set on his grandmother, who was sparring with a dragon over the fire pit. "That woman has no shame."

His mother and grandmother had been in an ongoing battle for longer than he'd been alive. Their families had been enemies for centuries and would never see eye-to-eye on most things. When his father had married his mother, there had been uproar about it in Hell. It was only because his dad had achieved the status of Lord of the Level that the marriage had been possible.

Kieron often romanticized their marriage. Like Romeo and Juliet, two houses had joined because of love. However, his mother often corrected him by telling him that love did not exist. It was lust, and—unlike Juliet—she could not kill herself to avoid her mother-in-law.

"Anika please, do you two always have to fight?" His father asked.

"If you prefer, I can fight with you instead?" His mother had a glint in her eyes that caused a shiver of fear to shoot down Kieron's spine. It became evident that the comment had a similar effect on his father when his face paled as the blood drained out of it.

"Why fight at all?" Dora asked. Kieron winced at the question.

His mother whipped her head around to stare at Dora, her short curls whipping around her face. She opened her mouth to speak, but luckily, Kieron's father put a hand on her arm and intercepted. "Dora, the more you become accustomed to Hell, the more you'll understand. Fighting is about power, and power is the most important commodity in Hell."

"I thought knowledge was power?" Dora said.

His father laughed and beamed a smile at Dora. "That it is! You can't fight well without knowledge."

Kieron narrowed his eyes at his father. He didn't like the look he was giving Dora. It happened when he spoke to her as if he enjoyed it or something. He knew he shouldn't be jealous, but when Dora smiled back at his father, he felt a possessive need to compete with him for her. "That's why you need to go to the academy, Dora. To gain knowledge and to learn to fight," he said.

When she pulled a face at him, he realized that he'd just said the most stupid thing ever. He expelled a sigh. *Idiot!* His heart hammered every time he was near her, but alas, she did not feel the same. *I will make her like me.* He told himself.

He pondered how he would achieve such a goal. He didn't think she'd enjoy being tied up in his dungeon for a hundred years, although his father had told him it worked on some girls. No, Dora was different, so his approach had to be different.

"Ah, my family all together." His grandmother's booming voice interrupted his thoughts. "And the family prude is here too, wonderful." She laughed at his mother, and Kieron winced with the knowledge of how this night would end.

"Ah Giganticor, I see you came to the party in your underwear again," Kieron's mother replied with a vicious look in her eyes.

"Well I can't wear too much, dear. You cover up so much, people forget what flesh looks like." His grandmother eyed the neck-to-toe emerald robes his mother was wearing. "Really dear, those robes look like curtains."

He could feel the heat of hatred coming off his mother in waves, literally as green smoke seeped out from under her robes. "Better curtains than being bombarded by your ancient flesh," his mother replied.

"Ha! If you've got it, flaunt it honey. If you're flabby wear a curtain—oh you already do." Kieron's grandmother countered.

Kieron gripped Dora's arm and slowly pulled her away from the group, ensuring they backed away an inch at a time. He knew what was coming.

"You know that thong is a yeast infection waiting to happen, don't you?" His mother snapped. "But, I suppose infection is a good thing in your family."

That had done it. She'd brought up Kieron's father's side of the family, and that never ended well.

His grandmother roared in outrage. She flicked his mother on the shoulder, knocking her backwards. "You dare to complain about my family? You little nobody!"

Kieron tightened his grip on Dora's arm and pulled her along with him as he ran for the door. Other demons at the barbeque noticed the fight, and they too made a beeline for the exit.

"Come on." He urged Dora to run with him.

"Shouldn't we stop them?" she asked.

Green smoke filled the room, and Lady Lascher's eyes glowed red.

"Trust me. The only people who get hurt in this are the bystanders." Kieron pulled Dora through the doorway as the sound of a loud explosion cracked through the air behind them. He peered back to see his grandmother slammed into a wall, causing a hairline crack to shoot up the plaster. "You dare to break things in *my* house?" His mother screamed at her.

Kieron yanked Dora out of the room and into the hallway. His father was the last to leave. He ran up behind them, slamming the doors to the ballroom shut after he left the room. Muffled sounds of breaking furniture and roars of pain could be heard through the closed doors.

He watched his father compose himself before he addressed the demons and partygoers in the hallway. "It's been lovely to see you all. Anika and I have really enjoyed tonight, but as with all good things, they must come to an end. We hope to see you at our next little shindig."

There were several pleasantries exchanged as people thanked his father for a wonderful barbeque before leaving. Meanwhile, the matriarchs of the Lascher family could be heard screaming and wailing at each other in the empty ballroom.

Kieron peeked at Dora. There was a confused expression on her face. He realized he was still gripping her arm and released her with a gentle pat. "Mother just likes to let off steam sometimes," he muttered.

"Green steam?" she asked, glancing at him with a look of horror.

"You two kids should go to your room." His father interrupted. "Given your delicate situation Dora, I don't think you're ready to face Lady Lascher yet," he added.

Dora smiled at him.

A possessive tug of jealousy spiked through Kieron again. He put his arm around her waist before turning towards his father. "I'll make sure nothing happens to her. She'll be fine with me."

"You need to improve your warrior skills before you're ready to protect anyone." His father scolded him.

*Wanker,* Kieron thought.

"I'm happy with avoidance for now. Let's go to your room, Kieron. We can listen to music or something." Dora smiled at him, causing his heart to do a little leap of joy.

"That sounds perfect," he replied. He grinned at his father as he led Dora away from him.

# 15

## BABY SIZED HORNS

Dora stared out of Kieron's bedroom window, taking in the view across the demonic city. Twisted castles were dotted around for miles with volcanoes of fire behind them lighting up the dark skies. *Is it always dark here?*

She peered down at the street below. Demons were skulking on dusty sidewalks, and the road was busy with fire-fuelled traffic. A strange sadness washed over her. *I don't belong here. I don't belong on Earth either—I don't belong anywhere.* She'd thought here at least, in a hellish dimension surrounded by ghouls and demons, she would finally belong. But the longer she was here, the more out of place she felt.

She watched an impish green demon push a large brown fluffy one off the sidewalk and into oncoming traffic. The brown fluffy demon splattered against the windshield of a souped-up Rolls Royce that was kitted out with lethal-looking spikes for spoilers. She watched the pieces of blood, guts and fur slide down the black Rolls. Anger burned in her throat. The green demon pointed and cackled at the fate of the fluffy one. *What did that poor demon ever do to anyone? Why attack it?*

Dora's knuckles whitened as she gripped the window ledge. She was fuming with anger at what she had just witnessed. She decided to go down there and push the green demon off the sidewalk. *See how he likes it! I will not stand by and witness other people suffering as if it is fucking entertainment.*

She paused because she realized she wasn't angry about one demon killing another—demons couldn't die in Hell. She was angry about what had been done to her. Her family and friends had tried to burn her alive, which was bad enough, but the worst part was that every single person in her world had been content to watch it happen. *They didn't do anything to stop it, not one of them!*

Dora wanted to cry, but she wasn't going to. She realized you couldn't trust anyone, not really. People only cared about themselves. There weren't any heroes in the world anymore. How many people chose to watch her go up in flames for entertainment? How many innocent souls suffered a similar fate every single day? If you were stuck with your back against the wall as the world was crumbling around you, the only person you could count on was yourself.

She was tired of being helpless in both worlds. Dungeons and funeral pyres be damned! She was going to make herself powerful so no one could ever do that to her again. She didn't want friends anymore. She wanted power.

"I brought cookies and milk." Kieron interrupted her thoughts as he came back into his room.

Dora lowered her head and sighed. *What about Kieron? He's a good friend.* She gritted her teeth. *Yeah? And how long will that last? You don't even know what he is.* A dark voice in the back of her mind shadowed her thoughts.

Still burning with anger and hatred for every other living thing in the universe, she turned to face Kieron. He appeared startled by her expression. *It must be pretty scary.*

"It's chocolate milk," he added, warily eyeing her up.

"What kind of demon are you, Kieron?" Her voice sounded dark even to her. It was cold and sharp.

He peered at his feet when he spoke. "I don't understand the question," he mumbled.

"Well, your mother is a terrifying green-smoky-thing, and your father is a massively frightening black-winged-thing. So what kind of demon are you?"

Kieron glared at her with narrowed eyes when she mentioned his father. "He's not frightening."

"He's pretty scary in demon form,"

"If you're into that kind of thing." Kieron folded his arms and scowled.

"Stop avoiding the question!" Dora snapped.

"I'm a Lascher demon," he mumbled, refusing to look at her as he placed the tray of cookies and chocolate milk onto the nightstand.

"What does a Lascher demon do?"

"Lots of things."

"Such as?"

"You know, stuff." His nostrils flared in anger. It was the first time she had seen him angry. His jaw clenched, and his eyes glittered with stormy shadows.

"Name one thing." She knew she was pushing him to tell her things he didn't want to, but she didn't care. *How can I trust him if he keeps me in the dark?*

"Magic," he snapped. "Okay, I can only do spells. I don't know why, and it's lame and useless. Are you happy now?"

"Yes, because you finally stopped lying to me! What's your demon form like?"

"It's terrifying."

"Show me it."

"No, it'll scare you." Kieron looked away.

"No it won't."

"I can't just turn it on. It's controlled by rage." He grumbled.

"I bet you don't even have a demon form." She taunted.

"Yes I do!" he cried as he stormed over to her. "And if you keep pushing me, you'll regret it." His voice deepened with menace.

"I doubt it." She really wanted to see his demon form, so she continued to piss him off. "I mean, if you even *have* a demon form."

His blue eyes sparkled with anger as his lips flattened into a grim line. He stood so close to her that she could feel the heat of his skin. "Fine, don't say I didn't warn you."

Dora stared in awe as his blue eyes turned red. The stormy ocean in them became burning fires. He let out a guttural growl, and goosebumps popped up on her arms. Her pulse raced as she stared up at him in awe.

Tiny black horns, just an inch high, grew on the top of his head and poked through his blond hair. They looked like shards of black glass. She watched them in awe, expecting them to grow larger, but they didn't.

"I told you, you would regret it," he said in a dark voice. It was his usual voice, but it sounded as if he was trying to imitate an ominous demon growl.

*Is he serious? That's how scary he gets—baby-sized horns and contact lenses.* Dora tried not to laugh. He was serious after all. But he was still Kieron, not some big, scary demon. She didn't have the heart to hurt his feelings. Of all the people she knew, he was the only decent one she'd ever met.

She decided to pretend to be scared, just for him and just this once. "Oh my!" She gasped and held her hand to her throat.

"You should not bring out my dark side, Dora." Demon-Kieron warned.

"Oh, I see that." She nodded, fighting to control the giggle inside her that tried to escape. "I'll never do it again. You're so big, strong and scary."

He gripped her shoulders with his hands and pulled her closer to him. "You should be scared, little one. I could do so many terrible things to you."

"Ah, um, okay then."

"Like this!" He kissed her. *What? I'm not that nice.* Dora tried to push him away, but changed her mind as his hot lips made the world melt away. It was like kissing heaven, but it made her skin burn. He groaned as his strong arms wrapped around her, pulling her closer to him. She forgot where she was and wrapped her arms around his broad shoulders, kissing him back with just as much passion.

He picked her up in his arms and made his way towards the bed. A shot of reality penetrated her mind. She pulled back from his kisses and looked into his now blue eyes. *I guess Demon-Kieron fades away if you kiss him.* "Er, what are you doing?" she asked.

"Making sweet love to you?" He appeared unsure.

"No, you're not." She told him.

"But it's what happens next," he said.

"No, it isn't."

"Don't you want to?"

"No. Well, probably not."

"We should try it and find out for certain." He attempted to persuade her.

"I'm pretty certain I don't want to. It's okay."

"Making sweet love is fun," he said. "You'll miss out on a good time."

"And teen pregnancy," she added with a fair amount of sarcasm. "I hear that's not as much fun."

"Okay, now I don't want to anyway. You ruined the moment," he muttered as he put her back on her feet.

"That's probably a good thing," she replied. Her heart raced, and her skin burned.

"Ohh, you're one of those kinds of girls." Kieron slapped himself in the forehead.

"What kind of girls?" she asked.

"You know. What are they called on Earth … frigid?"

"I am not!" Dora scowled at him.

"Maybe that's not the right word." He paused, and he appeared to think about it for a moment. "Will you go on a date with me tomorrow?"

"A date?"

"Yes, a nice one with me. I'll show you all the vilest places in Hell."

"How can a girl say no to that," Dora muttered.

"Is that a yes?"

"Yes, okay. I'll go on a date with you."

"Yay!" He grinned at her. "You won't regret it."

"Well, a demon date has to be more fun than a normal one, right?"

"Exactly! And Dora, did you at least learn something about demons from all of this?"

"Yep." She nodded and flashed a sweet smile. *They're all a bit silly,* she thought.

# POOEY

D ora smiled at Kieron as he led her through the saloon doors of a western-looking bar. Her skin tingled with warm jolts of pleasure when he squeezed her hand.

They made their way over to the huge red demon behind the bar. Dora widened her eyes in awe when she noticed the demon bartender. He had bulging muscles, large blood-colored horns and a goatee. *He looks like the devil.* She pulled back in a moment of hesitation as they neared the bar. The bar-demon glanced up at them with a scowl on his face.

"Are we allowed to drink here?" she whispered in Kieron's ear.

"Of course," he replied. "Look around you. This is an underage bar."

She glanced around the room and froze. Her jaw dropped open with shock at what she saw. A demon resembling a five-year old girl sat at the table next to them.

She took a loud sip from a bottle of whiskey through a straw. Some preteens were playing poker in a nearby booth. Meanwhile, at the back of the room a group of toddlers appeared to be having a kegger.

"Isn't that dangerous for them?" Dora asked.

"Not really. They're demons. They don't have livers, and statistically drunken adults act childish, but drunk children tend to remain the same as they are when sober. The bar fights are much less violent as a result," Kieron replied.

Dora found it hard to watch a child drinking whiskey. It was even weirder to see the tween-aged, gangster-looking kid at the back of the room smoking Al Capone's. "It just seems so wrong," she said.

"Seeing a sixty year old woman dressed in leopard skin spandex and dancing to Britney Spears—now that's just wrong."

She nodded. *Fair point, it is very disturbing to see that.*

They reached the bar and waited for the bar-demon to come over. He put down the glass he was polishing and walked over to them, wearing a scowl.

"A bottle of Jack Daniels and two glasses," Kieron said.

The bar-demon grunted and slammed two shot glasses and a bottle of Jack on the bar. "That'll be two dark soul-chips," the bar-demon replied.

Kieron handed over two sparkling gems. They looked like smoky diamonds, and they glowed with a faint gray light. The bar-demon took the gems and dropped them into the register.

Kieron picked up the bottle and the glasses before leading Dora to a table near the windows.

"What were those gems?" she asked.

"It's the currency here," he said. "The darker the chip, the less it's worth. Um, imagine a dark soul-chip is a five-dollar bill, and a light soul-chip is a fifty-dollar bill. If you have a white soul-chip, well, you can buy a castle with it. They're really rare."

"Why don't you use dollars instead?" she asked.

"These." He held up a smoky gem. "Are pieces of people's souls. The more souls you have, the more power you have. The lighter the soul, the more powerful it is."

Dora gasped. "So my soul—"

"Should never to be mentioned in public for your own good." Kieron briefly scanned the room.

She nodded with a shiver. She didn't know what color her soul was, but judging by the way Kieron acted, it must be one of the lighter shades.

"But didn't the truck driver find my soul disgusting, though?" she asked.

"Think of it as stinky cheese. It's a delicacy in small pieces, but you don't want a lump of it sitting next to you."

"So I'm like stinky cheese?" She narrowed her eyes at him. "Way to go Casanova."

"You know I met him once," Kieron replied, missing the point. "I wasn't supposed to because he ended up on the other side."

"The other side of what?"

"You know. The other 'H' place."

"Oh, you mean Heave—"

Kieron slapped his hand over her mouth and gagged her with it. A poker playing teen winked at them and wiggled his eyebrows.

"Don't say that word here," he whispered.

"Mmmay." She attempted to reply, but decided to nod instead.

He removed his hand and rubbed her shoulder. "Sorry, it's just there are some things you can't say here."

"Okay, I get it. Thanks I guess, but I have another question."

Kieron groaned while pouring them both a drink.

"The truck driver knew about my soul, so why is keeping it a secret so important? If he can see it, can't everyone?"

"Oh, it's only because he's related to Charon." He waved the question away with his hand.

"Sharon? Who's Sharon?" Dora frowned, trying to work out who he meant.

"C-H-A-R-O-N, the ferryman. Not Sharon the happy hairdresser!"

"Ohh," she said, still not entirely sure who Charon was. "Wasn't he in Percy Jackson?"

Kieron slapped his hand to his forehead and sighed. "Yes, that guy."

"Okay, so are lots of people related to Charon here?"

"No, there are only a few on the Highway to Hell. And, before you ask, none of them were in Percy Jackson!"

Dora grinned. She loved it when she made Kieron squirm. He shot her an impatient look, and she bit the inside of her cheek to keep from laughing while watching him fumble over the answers. "The books or the movie?" she asked, innocently taking a sip of her drink.

"Both. I mean neither. They're not in fiction anywhere!"

"Not even in Dante's Inferno?" Dora's grin widened when his face became animated with frustration.

"Don't even get me started on that book," he muttered and slugged down his drink in one shot. "Come on. Let's go to the fair. It'll keep you amused."

"Ooh, that sounds fun." She stood up before turning to Kieron with a wink. "Not that this wasn't entertaining."

He replied with an ominous growl before putting his hand around her waist and guiding her to the exit.

Dora stood at the counter of the 'Shoot 'Em Up' stand in the Demonique Fayre. She peered up at the garish colored stand. Fluffy demons hung from a rack, emitting helpless squeaks and squirming to be free. The brightly painted sign above the mini demons read; 'Win a Cuddly Toy'.

Kieron was concentrating hard as he stared through the sight of the crossbow, taking aim at the target on the back of a marketing executive's head. He had promised her he would win her a cuddly toy, but to be honest she wasn't sure she wanted a cute, helpless demon—although they were adorable.

"So the banks here are full of stinky cheese?" Dora blurted as Kieron released the trigger on the crossbow. Her question made him jump as he took the shot. The arrow wobbled in the air, darting at a skewed angle before embedding in the rotund backside of a marketing executive. She sniggered. He'd hit the guy who had invented ring tones.

Kieron scowled at her. "You did that on purpose."

"Maybe." She flashed him a sweet smile. "Is it my turn now?"

"Yes." He took a step back. His eyes narrowed to slits as he gestured for her to take her turn.

She glanced back at Kieron. She didn't trust him. She was certain he was going to do something behind her back. He stood behind her with his arms folded, staring intently at her. When he noticed her looking, he arched an eyebrow at her in a challenging manner.

Dora shrugged at him and turned to face the weapon. She bent over the crossbow and peered through the sight, aiming at the nearest target. Her target of choice was the man who had sold cancerous food to kittens via marketing. She aimed the arrow at the center of the large round target on his back and prepared to pull the trigger.

She jumped and gritted her teeth when Kieron's large, warm hand slapped her on the ass and remained there. *Oh, nice try loser.* She ignored his hand when it squeezed her backside and took the shot anyway. The arrow hit the target, dead center. The marketing executive exploded with a pop, splattering blood and guts

116

all over the other targets.

Dora straightened up and glanced back at Kieron's hand, which was still on her ass.

"Ahem," she said.

"What?" He looked innocent.

"Remove your hand, or I'll shoot you in the ass." She picked up the crossbow and threatened him with it.

"Oh!" He looked down and removed his hand, wearing an innocent expression. "I don't know how that got there."

"Sure you don't," she said, shaking her head.

"No, reall—"

"A cuddly toy for the lovely lady," the carnie demon said. He was a blue demon with perfect abs and little horns. Judging by his face and horn size, Dora guessed he was a teenage demon.

"Which one do you want?" the carnie demon asked.

Dora examined the rows of tiny, cute demons. Some were fluffy, and others had big sad eyes. Most of them were wriggling and squeaking at her. "Pick meeeee, pick meeeee!"

However, one of them was hanging limply from its hook. It was a pooey brown-colored demon with straggly fur and a squashed face. It stared at its feet and mumbled to itself. Dora strained to hear its words over the happy begging demons, blocking out the high-pitched squeals to hear what this one was mumbling.

"No one ever picks me." It grumbled.

"I'll take that one." She pointed to the straggly defeatist demon.

The carnie widened his eyes in surprise. "Are you sure?"

"Yep." She nodded. *The little fella looks as if he needs some hope.*

The carnie shrugged, lifted the grumpy demon off its hook and handed it to Dora.

She peered at the prize in her hands. The little guy was only about a foot tall, and he was still grumbling. "Only picked me out of pity." He complained.

"Exactly." Dora told him. "And now you're my pet, and I'm going to have to name you."

"Why bother? You'll probably eat me next week." He grumbled at her, folding his arms in a huff.

"I'm not going to eat you." Dora put him on her shoulder.

He held onto her hair so he wouldn't fall off. "Not even good enough for dinner," he mumbled in her ear.

"What are you going to call ... er, it?" Kieron asked.

"I'm doomed, why bother?" it muttered.

"Pooey," she said. "His name is Pooey."

"Oh great, now I feel even more like shit," Pooey said.

# 17

## A DEAL WITH DADDY

Kieron smiled as he walked down the endless halls of Castle Lascher. He'd had a fantastic date with Dora last night and was pleased she was finally enjoying Hell. He'd worried at first because there had been a melancholy look in her eyes since her parents had tried to burn her, but on the date she'd been playful and fun again. Oddly, even the defeatist demon, Pooey, cheered her up. He complained and made her giggle a lot.

Kieron followed the lit torches to his father's office door. He paused outside of it and frowned with concern. He had a daunting suspicion his father had summoned him here to talk about Dora. It was Sunday today, which was one of his father's busiest days in the office, so Kieron assumed he'd been summoned here about something important.

He knocked on the mahogany door, and the bang echoed through the castle.

"Enter," his father shouted.

Kieron pushed open the door before stepping into the large onyx chamber. At the center of the room, he found his father sitting behind a granite desk on a steel throne. The high back of the chair loomed around Lord Lascher like an intricately carved frame.

Kieron glanced at the thick iron doors of the family vault behind his father. Magic swirled around the closed vault door in the form of purple and green smoke. He knew from experience that the curses engraved on it were unbreakable, magical locks.

He walked over to the desk and took a seat opposite his father, glancing down at the blood-signed scrolls and piles of dark soul-chips littering the surface before peering up at his father, who watched him with interest over his glasses. Lord Lascher studied Kieron in silence for a few moments before removing his glasses and placing them on the desk. Kieron recognized his father's sharp black suit, and the devilish gleam in his eyes. *He looks as if he means business today.*

"I got your summons." Kieron broke the silence.

"Yes, I see," his father replied, giving nothing away.

"What do you want?" Kieron wanted to go back to hanging out with Dora and had no patience for his father's games today.

"It's about Dora," his father said. "She will be starting school tomorrow, and I thought we should discuss the long terms plans for her."

A bubble of panic expanded in his chest. Long-term plans in Hell tended to mean eternity.

"What are your thoughts?" Kieron asked in the

calmest voice he could manage. *Please let her stay.*

"I'd like to make her stay with us more permanent."

Kieron frowned. It was what he wanted, but he didn't like the look in his father's eyes. "Why?"

"I like her. She's a nice girl. You two make a cute couple, and I approve of her for you." His father smiled, and the tips of his fangs slid over his bottom lip.

It was everything Kieron wanted to hear, and that worried him. In Hell especially, if it sounded too good to be true, it usually was.

"That's good," Kieron replied, after careful consideration. "But she can't stay in Hell forever as a human."

His father waved the comment away. "We'll worry about that when we come to it. For now, we need to get her past Judgment Day, and to do that we need her to start learning evil."

Kieron nodded in agreement, but there was a sinking feeling in his chest. It was okay when he had been sneaking Dora into Hell, but his father's sudden interest in her worried him. *It could be jealousy because I don't like how he looks at Dora. No, that makes no sense. He just said he wanted Dora to stay to be with me. I agree with everything he's saying, so why is this conversation creeping me out?*

"Why do you want Dora to stay in Hell?" Kieron blurted out. He'd never been very subtle.

"Because she'll straighten you out!" His father bellowed.

Kieron sat back in his chair in shock. "What?"

"She's perfect for you. When you're with her, you break the rules, you get in trouble and you use magic like a demon should. For years I've worried you'll get kicked out of Hell with all your caring and worrying, but with her around you act like a true Lascher. She's making you into a demon I can be proud of." Red fire burned in his father's eyes as he spoke with passion. After a few moments, he calmed down. His eyes simmered down to dark blue. "And, I like her. She'll be a wonderfully fun daughter-in-law," he added with a smile.

"Okaaaaay." Kieron stretched out the word while he considered his father's comments. He had never connected with his father, not that his father hadn't tried.

Fishing trips had turned into battles of will over the souls they fished out of the lava, always beginning with an inevitable argument about whether the souls should be returned to the drink or saved. Of course, Kieron had always wanted to save them, which had disgusted his father.

This was the first time he and his father had agreed on anything, and maybe that was the problem. More than anything else in the world, Kieron wanted Dora to stay in Hell with him. But if his father wanted it, he wondered if it was the wrong thing to do.

"So, um, what happens to Dora if she learns to be better at evil?" Kieron asked, attempting to sound casual about it.

"She takes the test and passes. Then she can stay in Hell," his father replied just as casually. But he didn't look Kieron in the eye, he peered at one of the scrolls on his desk instead.

"So, she'll stay in Hell as a human with a soul?" Kieron asked, still unsure of the details.

"Hmm." His father nodded.

"Was that a yes?" Kieron persisted.

"That was a yes, yes."

Kieron smiled, but a moment later he narrowed his eyes with suspicion. "The 'yes' I said was a yes, but was the 'hmm' you said a yes?"

"My boy, you're making no sense." His father continued reading the scroll and smiled.

Kieron scowled. "Will Dora's soul be safe?" He demanded.

"Yes," his father said.

Kieron sighed, but he couldn't shift the uneasy feeling in the pit of his stomach. After a few seconds, he wondered if this was another trick. "Will it be safe inside her body?"

"Hmm?" His father took no notice of him.

"Her soul, will it be safe in her body?"

"For the time being, yes," his father replied.

"What do you mean *for the time being*?" Kieron's scowl deepened.

"She's human. They all die eventually, you know."

Kieron sighed. That was true. Humans didn't live for very long. Perhaps she was better off in Hell, after all. *At least here she'll never die.*

"Okay, I'll try and help her do well at the Academy tomorrow," he eventually said.

"Good, good. I'll help too, in my own way."

"What does that mean?"

"Oh, you know, study guides and things." The vague wave of his hand made Kieron worry again.

"I've got all these contracts to go over, so that'll be all for today." His father dismissed him.

Kieron stared at his father for a few more seconds before standing and walking out of the room, feeling uncertain about everything. He shut the office door behind him, glancing briefly at his father before it closed. His father's eyes glittered as he watched him leave the chamber.

In the gloomy hallway, Kieron tried to make sense of the confusing conversation. On one hand, he wanted Dora to stay because she made him happy. He didn't know if she made him a better demon, but he knew he was happy when he was near her. On the other hand, he didn't trust his father or anyone in Hell. Dora didn't belong here. If she stayed, would she remain the same? Would she remain human?

The more he thought about it, the more confusing it all became. In the end, it was easier to stick to what he did know. He knew Dora was good, and that wouldn't change. Now he knew she was going to be able to stay with him, which was a good thing, right?

Kieron walked down the corridor towards her room, his smile back in place as he thought about seeing her, but the skin on his arms prickled with goosebumps. Something wasn't right.

# 18

## DAEMON ACADEMIA

"Come on, Pooey. It's not my fault!" Dora called out. "I don't have time for this," she muttered, looking under her bed. *Where is he?*

"I'm not staying here." Pooey's sad voice echoed through her bedroom.

"I can't take you with me. I have to go to school today." Dora sighed. Pooey had been cute all weekend until he found out she was leaving him to go to school this morning.

"If you leave me here, they'll eat me alive!" Pooey cried.

"No, they won't. I'm sure they won't." She frowned. She wasn't entirely sure Pooey would be safe here. Lady Lascher had given him a funny look when Dora had brought him home.

The clock on the nightstand ticked louder than normal. Dora knew she only had a few minutes before she had to set off. *Screw it.* "Okay, here's the deal, Pooey," she said, peering around the room. "You can come with me *if* you can find somewhere to hide, so no one can see you."

Pooey's head popped up out of the side pocket of her backpack. "Will this do?"

"How the hell did you get in there?" She blinked in amazement. She'd been packing the bag when he went missing and had no idea how he'd managed to hide in it.

"Ninja skills," he said in a bored voice.

Dora laughed and picked up the bag. She threw it over her shoulder and shook her head. "Great, a Pooey ninja. Okay, let's go to school." She let out a sigh. *Today is gonna suck.*

Dora turned when she heard a light knock at the door. It opened to reveal Kieron standing in the doorway, wearing a black robe. He looked ominous and almost scary under the dark hood. "Where's your robe?" he asked. "You can't go dressed like that!" His panicked expression made him appear less frightening and much cuter.

"Oh, we have to wear the uniform?" Dora asked, glancing down at her new black miniskirt and blood-red pantyhose.

"Yes." He nodded several times as if to establish the importance of it.

"Can I put it on over my clothes?"

"Yeah, just make sure you're wearing it or the professors go ballistic."

"Okay." She dropped her bag off her shoulder and

onto the floor, wincing when she heard a tiny 'oof' sound coming from the bag. "Sorry," she mumbled as she draped the heavy black robe over her clothes.

"It's okay," Kieron replied, clearly unaware she had been apologizing to Pooey.

"Does it look okay?" She spun around with her robe swishing around her ankles.

"Perfect." He winked at her. "Let's get going. They do awful things to you if you're late."

"Okay." Dora grabbed her bag and swung it over her shoulder.

"Oh, don't do that, or I'm gonna barf." Pooey's tiny voice grumbled.

"What?" Kieron asked.

Dora coughed. "Huh? Oh, I just had a tickle in my throat," she attempted to cover-up Pooey's complaints.

Kieron narrowed his eyes and shot her a suspicious glance before nodding and turning to leave the room. She shivered as she followed him. The first day of school— even outside of Hell, it sounded frightful.

Kieron gazed across the classroom at Dora. *Why is she studying her nails? Crap! Is she even paying attention?*

They were sitting in Professor Kazaik's class studying power and persuasion. It was one of the most important classes in the curriculum. There were two reasons why this was the class Dora needed to pay attention to. Firstly, Kazaik was beyond evil. He'd cut her head off if she didn't know the answer. Secondly, it was the subject most likely to be on the exams.

A knot of worry tightened in Kieron's stomach, making him feel sick. If Dora got her head cut off for messing around in class today it wouldn't grow back! His worry became panic when she yawned and studied her fingernails instead of the blackboard. *I should have sat next to her, damn it!*

"If pure evil comes from power, how do we attain it?" Professor Kazaik asked the class.

The entire class stared at him, giving him their full attention, except for Dora. She appeared to be drawing a smiley face on her middle finger instead.

Kazaik's black eyes settled on Dora with a dangerous glint in them.

Kieron helplessly watched in silence. *Please, please look up.*

Dora didn't look up. She grinned at her finger artwork and wiggled it at herself.

Kazaik narrowed his eyes and pressed his lips together until they became a thin line. He was a tall and pale man with long black hair whipping around him in snaking tendrils. He was the highest warlock in the level. Dark magic flowed through every inch of him. As a master of magic, he could do just about anything. He was a first class professor of power, which meant he was the most powerful demon in the school.

Kieron's stomach muscles clenched in fear as Kazaik strode down the row of desks towards Dora. Magic swirled in the air around him, leaving a trail of blood-red smoke in his wake.

He stopped at Dora's desk, staring down at her with fire burning in his eyes.

Dora must have noticed the shadow over her desk because she raised her head and peered up at him.

"Oh, hello," she said.

Kieron groaned. *How am I going to get her out of here if she messes up?* The answer was simple; he would have to get his head cut off instead. He sighed. Being in lust was not easy.

"The answer, Ms. Carridine." Kazaik snapped. He curled his bony fingers into fists.

*I'm going to have to do something soon.* Kieron tried to think of a way to distract Kazaik.

"Um, the question was about evil, right?" Dora flashed an innocent expression.

Kieron's heart sank. *He won't fall for that.*

"If pure evil comes from power, how do we attain it?" Kazaik repeated.

Kieron was about to stand up and shout out the answer, but Dora did the strangest thing. She rested her head on her bag. *What's she doing?*

Kieron watched her in awe as she nodded before lifting her head back up and looking directly at Kazaik. "We attain power through hate," Dora said in a confident tone. She frowned for a moment as if contemplating her answer. "Does that mean if I want to be all powerful, all I need to do is hate something enough?"

Kieron blinked. It was profound. It was a simplistic answer. It was correct! He glanced at Kazaik. The professor was smiling. Kazaik never smiled, and the smile looked twisted on his face.

"Good answer," Kazaik said. "Does drawing on yourself help you listen?"

"It seems to." Dora nodded, waving her middle finger at him.

*Did she just flip him off?*

"I'm not often surprised. You're not quite the idiot I first thought you were." Kazaik turned on his heel and walked back to the front of the class.

Kieron breathed a sigh of relief. He stared at Dora in awe. *How did she know the answer? How did she get away with flipping him off?*

Kazaik turned and faced the class. His eyes burned red as they focused on Dora. "Since our newest student is so well informed, I think she can show us her power. Ms. Carridine, come here please."

"Er, what for?" She sounded reluctant.

"I'd like you demonstrate the use of power. Clearly you have mastered your hate, so it will be a good example for the class to see it in action." Kazaik's smile never reached his eyes.

*Aww fuck, he's going to make her cast a spell.*

Kieron gripped his desk as he watched Dora stand up and walk to the front of the class with her head held high. *I hope she knows what she's doing.*

"What kind of example?" she asked.

Kazaik pointed to the grimoire on his desk. "A simple curse will do, I think. Can you curse someone here for me?"

Dora shrugged and walked over to the grimoire. "I can try." She glanced down at the spell book and frowned. "There might be a problem though."

"Such as?" Kazaik raised an eyebrow at her.

"I can't read Latin. This looks like Latin." She slowly flipped through the book. "Is there a translated version I can work with?"

"What do you mean *you can't read Latin*?" Kazaik sounded appalled. "How are you even in this class if you can't read the language of sorcery?"

"Um, I dunno?"

Kazaik shot her a disgusted look. "Bloody new-age witches," he muttered as he waved his arm in the air and summoned a translated copy of the grimoire from the stock room at the back of the class.

Dora smiled in awe as the book traveled through the air towards her. She caught it in her hands with a grin. "That was great! Do it again."

Kazaik appeared upset by her request. "I will not."

"Awwwww."

"Don't ever make that noise in my classroom again." An expression of abject horror passed over Kazaik's impassive face.

Kieron had to hold in a giggle. Dora was confusing the crap out of him.

"Okay so, who do you want me to curse, and with what?" she asked.

"Anyone here with anything you like." An evil smile spread across Kazaik's face. He obviously didn't think Dora could do anything.

*Neither do I,* Kieron thought.

"Oh, I don't need a book for that." Dora dropped the book on the desk.

"Really? You are a proficient witch, are you?" Kazaik sounded unconvinced.

"Yes, I like to think so."

"Show us."

Dora's gaze traveled around the classroom until her eyes locked on Kieron. She winked at him. The bubble of panic in his stomach grew. *Oh no! What's she going to do now?* She spun on her heel and stared at Kazaik with anger in her eyes. "Fireknackers!"

Kazaik's underwear ignited into a fiery blaze. Shocked students jumped to their feet as the blaze grew around Kazaik's groin. He peered down as the flames licked around his legs. He didn't utter a word, but his eyes were watering.

"Dowzer," he muttered. The ceiling opened up and several gallons of water fell through the opening, drenching him and dousing the flames. The room fell silent with only dripping sounds coming from the soggy professor. Dark smoke billowed around him, which could have been from the fire or Kazaik himself.

The bell rang as class ended, but no one moved. All the students were staring in awe at their teacher.

"A good use of hate, Ms. Carridine," Kazaik muttered. "Class dismissed."

Dora returned to her desk for her bag. Kieron grabbed her arm and pulled her out of the classroom as quickly as he could. All the other students were in a hurry to leave as they stampeded towards the door. The air was pregnant with danger, like a balloon filled with acid that was about to explode.

"Did I do okay?" Dora asked as they left the room.

Kieron stared at her hopeful expression, feeling a sudden urge to hug her and strangle her at the same time. "You did wonderfully," he said instead. He glanced back at Kazaik who was scowling at Dora's back. "Now we need to teach you to ward off curses before the next class," he added.

Dora dropped her bag on her bed with a sigh.

"Shit!" Pooey cried.

"Oh crap." Dora unzipped the pocket and let Pooey out of the bag. "Sorry."

"Why not just bash my head in with your fist? It'll hurt less." Pooey grumbled as he crawled out of her bag.

"Sorry, it was a long day. I kept forgetting you were in there."

"You remembered when you needed the answers." Pooey put his hands on his hips.

"You were a total lifesaver."

"I know," he said.

Dora sat on the bed next to him. "I think I'm doomed. How am I going to do this all again tomorrow?"

"You're starting to sound like me."

She smiled. "How do you know so much about magic and evil?"

"I read a lot."

"I guess I read the wrong books."

"Try this one." Pooey dropped the translated grimoire from Professor Kazaik's class into her lap.

"How did you get this?" She picked up the book, staring at Pooey in awe.

"I'm a ninja." He shrugged.

"You think I can learn all this in one night?" She flipped through the pages and grimaced at the book.

"If you can't, you're fucked," he replied. "You're probably fucked."

Kieron burst into the room with his arms filled with books. He wore a determined expression as he kicked the door shut behind him and dropped the books onto the floor. "We need to give you a crash course in evil." He declared.

"Do you think we can do it in one night?" Dora winced. It appeared to be an impossible task.

"We have to," Kieron replied. He flashed a winning smile. "Don't worry. You'll be an expert in evil by the end of tonight."

Pooey rolled his eyes.

# DOODLYSQUAT

Dora rubbed her bleary eyes and yawned. She, Kieron and Pooey had been awake for most of the night practicing evil spells and curses. She was certain she'd memorized at least three books worth of spells, but the spells weren't powerful enough when she cast them. Even Kieron's were stronger, which wasn't a good thing since he'd admitted he didn't have much power as a demon.

Kieron gripped her hand as they strolled into Kazaik's classroom. She glanced up at Kieron and noticed a worried frown knitting his eyebrows together. He had told her about the kinds of things Kazaik did in his classroom, and for the first time, she worried too. She had set the guy's ass on fire, which probably hadn't been her wisest decision. According to Kieron, Kazaik was a big fan of revenge. *Oh, joy.*

Kazaik displayed a pleasant smile when she walked into his classroom. The smile never reached his black eyes.

She hurried to her desk and sat down. She glanced at Kieron when he chose the desk next to her. He gave her a reassuring smile, making her feel more secure. *It'll be okay. Kieron's with me.*

"That is not your seat, Mr. Lascher." Kazaik snapped at Kieron.

"I ... er, but the view of the blackboard is better from here," Kieron replied.

"In this class, seats are assigned. Now back to your usual place." Kazaik waved his hand. Both Kieron and his desk blew across the classroom, smashing into the far wall.

Dora jumped up to run to Kieron's aid, but an invisible force slammed into her shoulders and pushed her back down into her seat. She struggled against it, glancing up at Kazaik. Amusement lit up his eyes. *He's enjoying watching me struggle like a mortal.*

"Releashai," she muttered. The invisible force pushing her downwards disappeared. She stood up and glared at Kazaik.

He appeared surprised for a moment until a dark scowl settled on his face. "I see you would like to demonstrate your skills in sorcery again, Ms. Carridine."

She glanced across the room at Kieron, who struggled to his feet as he pulled broken pieces of desk off him. Splinters littered his torn robe, and he had a nasty-looking scratch down his left cheek. He caught her eye and shook his head with a sense of urgency.

"Sure, why not?" Dora scowled at Kazaik. She knew it was a stupid idea, but he had annoyed her by hurting Kieron like that. *It's about time I practiced these spells, and here's the perfect asshole to try them out on.*

"Today class, we're going to have a demonstration in defense," Kazaik said, wearing a grim smile. "Come up to the front of the class please, Ms. Carridine."

She gritted her teeth and walked towards Kazaik. She shot Kieron a sideways glance. He shook his head with concern knotting his brow.

*Don't worry. I can do this.* She smiled at Kieron and straightened her shoulders. She stopped beside the professor and waited to see what he had in store for her.

"Since you're adept at the basic skills in sorcery, today we're going to see what kind of curses you can repel." Kazaik smiled as he turned to face her.

"So basically, you're going to attack me?" Dora narrowed her eyes at him.

"Yes." He grinned with devilish delight.

"Bring it on." She faced him, mulling over the defensive spells she had learnt. Countering a spell often involved casting a curse of another kind, instead of a lame protection spell. The best defense was offense. Dora knew she could be incredibly offensive if she wanted to be. It was all about the choice of the spell, not the power of it. *If I choose the right spells, he's going down.*

"Incinerato!" Kazaik cried. Flames burst out of the palms of his hands and shot towards her.

She jumped back, narrowly avoiding the fireballs. "Doodlysquat!" she cried out in retaliation.

A ton of manure dropped through the ceiling and landed on Kazaik, dousing his flaming hands and burying him under a mound of horseshit. She heard a growl from within the pile of manure and suppressed the urge to laugh. *That was just great!*

The earth trembled under her feet when giant, hairy arms poked through the top of the manure. A massive monkey, wearing Kazaik's robes, crawled out of the pile of dung. It scooped up a lump of excrement and rolled it into a massive ball.

"Sizero," the monkey chattered. The manure ball shrank to the size of a basketball.

*Oh no you don't.* "Nothrowpoo!" Dora cried. The monkey fell under her control, and its wicked glare transformed into a blank stare.

She grinned. "Facepalm," she said. The monkey splatted the ball of manure into its own face and rubbed it in. *This is so easy,* she thought, feeling a bit cocky.

"Truform." The Kazaik monkey growled. He changed back into a man who was dirtied with manure. He spat some of it out of his mouth and looked up at her with a murderous expression. "Guilloti!" Kazaik snarled.

Dora yelped as an invisible force flung her onto the professor's desk. Thick leather straps wrapped over her whole body, binding her to the table.

"Mmmfn." She tried to cast a curse through the leather gag, but nothing came out. Her eyes widened in horror when she saw the sharp guillotine blade hovering in the air over her neck. *Oh shit!*

"You see Ms. Carridine, not all curses can be deflected with bullshit." Kazaik wore a nasty smile.

*Horseshit,* she thought.

"Decaperato!" he cried. The blade dropped. She

screamed under the gag, and her heart jumped into her mouth.

"Haltus." The blade stopped a few millimeters from her neck. She couldn't turn her head to look up, but she recognized the voice.

Lord Lascher stepped into her line of vision, offering a polite smile to Kazaik. "Sorry to interrupt professor, but I need to take Dora and Kieron out of class today—family emergency."

"We were just finishing off this lesson. Is it possible for Dora to finish her presentation first?" Kazaik asked. The blade of the guillotine wobbled and touched the skin on her neck. The sharp edge of the guillotine sliced her skin, drawing a bloody line across her throat.

"I'm afraid not. It's an urgent matter." Lord Lascher flashed a warm smile at the professor. "Releashai," he muttered. The guillotine and leather straps evaporated, allowing Dora to sit up on the desk.

"Grab your bags kids. We need to get going."

She climbed off the professor's table. "Thanks," she muttered to Lord Lascher as she walked past him and headed for her desk.

"Dora isn't a member of the Lascher family, is she?" Kazaik scowled at her as she picked up her backpack. She crossed the room to meet Kieron in the doorway.

"She will be soon." Lord Lascher smiled again. "I apologize for the interruption." He gave a short bow in Kazaik's direction before walking towards her and Kieron and leading them out of the classroom.

"Lucky timing." Dora smiled at Lord Lascher once

they left the classroom.

"Luck has nothing to do with it." Lord Lascher grinned.

"What does that mean?" Kieron narrowed his eyes.

"Oh, nothing, just you will both be my students from now on. We don't want Dora losing her head, do we?"

"No, but what kind of tuition are we getting? You're not a professor." Kieron found his father's help more alarming than Kazaik's threats. Dora didn't understand what he was worrying about. Lord Lascher had saved her ass a couple of times now. There was no reason to fear him.

"You, my lucky students, will have the pleasure of practical training in Hell." Lord Lascher winked.

"What, in the punishment sectors?" Kieron's eyes widened, and his voice was brimming with awe.

"Yes. I've been given permission to let you kids go in there, and I'm allowed to show you true evil. Think of it as work experience."

"Work?" Dora lost any enthusiasm she might have had over it when she heard that word. "That er, sounds like work."

"Trust me. Once you've worked in Hell, the word has a whole new meaning." Lord Lascher told her.

Kieron nodded with excitement lighting up his eyes.

*It's gotta be better than losing my head, right?* "Okay, let's go to work, I guess …"

# 20
## CORPORATE HELL

Cheerful music filled the elevator as it dropped through several levels of Hell at breakneck speed. Dora glanced at Lord Lascher. He was humming along in time to the music and tapping his feet. The music was similar to something her grandmother would listen to, and it was making her feel queasy from the sugary sweetness of it. She peered at Kieron. He was swaying in time to the music too.

She stared at the steel doors in front of her with a blank feeling of disbelief, painfully aware of the Lascher's both swaying in synchronization on either side of her. *It's like a Brady Bunch nightmare in here.*

She frowned and slyly kicked Kieron in the shin. He yelped and glared at her, fortunately losing his unity with the elevator music. She sighed with relief, pulling an innocent expression.

"Oww, what was that for?" Kieron frowned at her.

"Sanity," she replied.

The elevator dinged and came to an abrupt halt, causing her to lose her balance and fall against Kieron. He caught her in his arms when she landed against his muscled chest. She glanced up at him, and he grinned down at her. His hot skin burned her fingers through his white shirt. *Why does he always have to be so hot?* She blinked at the thought. The contact made her skin heat up too. *Think clean thoughts. Think clean thoughts ...*

"Ahem." Lord Lascher glanced at them, making a fake coughing sound.

Dora flinched and jumped back out of Kieron's reach. She straightened her shoulders in an attempt to hide the burning embarrassment flushing her cheeks. *Awkward!*

The elevator doors slid open to reveal a large office with gray carpet tiles on the floor and beige wallpaper on the walls. It looked like any other office in the universe with small cubicles lining it in endless rows. Each cubicle held an office worker. Some were human-looking and others were demons, but all were dressed in business suits or uniform T-shirts bearing the company logo. The T-shirts were red polo-shirts with the company logo emblazoned across them. The logo was a picture of a fireball with the words 'Corporate Hell' stamped beneath it.

Dora glanced back at Lord Lascher. He smiled, spreading out his arms and gesturing for her and Kieron to step out of the elevator and into the office. "Welcome to Corporate Hell."

She and Kieron stepped into the office, side-by-side.

Lord Lascher followed before overtaking them to lead them on a tour of his department. She glanced at Kieron and noticed he appeared as disappointed as she felt. Corporate Hell looked immensely boring.

"Corporate Hell is one of the most productive sectors here," Lord Lascher said, smoothing out his black jacket and adjusting his red tie.

Dora peered at the office workers as she passed them. A bald guy in a navy suit was trying to balance a pencil on his nose. He failed, and the pencil rolled off his nose and clattered onto the desk in front of him. He picked it up and started doing the same thing all over again.

"We do exciting and innovative work here ..." Lord Lascher continued.

Dora spotted a woman in her twenties, staring at her computer monitor in a demented fashion. She ferociously chewed on her own fingernails, down to the cuticle.

"Our secret is to provide a happy work environment for our staff." Lord Lascher appeared oblivious to the middle-aged man in the corner cubicle, who had leapt out of his chair and was screaming at his monitor. Dora watched in awe as the man took a baseball bat and swung it at the screen with hate-driven force. The computer screen shattered in an explosion of plastic pieces, and he jumped up and down on its remains, having a tantrum.

"That's gotta be a home run," she muttered.

"Job satisfaction, that's the key." Lord Lascher continued, leading them on the guided tour of the room, appearing oblivious to the insanity around him.

Kieron gasped when they passed two secretaries who

were fighting over the photocopier. A tall blonde held a shorter redhead by the hair as she banged her head against the top of the machine. Meanwhile, the redhead shot staples into the blonde's hand with a giant stapler. "It's my fucking turn, you bitch!" the redhead cried.

"We find our workers are most productive in a competitive environment," Lord Lascher said before he pointed to the wall behind him.

Dora spun around to see a white board mounted against a windowed partition. The board had a table drawn on it with headings of 'Staff' and 'Souls'. The staff column held a list of names. Next to each name was a number written in blood. She widened her eyes when the numbers changed on their own. "What do they get if they win?" she asked.

"Ah, a good question. They win the company bonus," Lord Lascher said.

"What's that?" Dora studied the board, watching the top name constantly change.

"A bottle of wine."

"But can't they just conjure a bottle of wine?" she asked.

"Yes, but that's not the point. Winning is the point."

"But you don't win anything."

"It's the same theory as video games. How many hours do people spend working for nothing in a video game, and to what end? The win is the ultimate prize."

"But you don't win anything." Dora repeated.

Kieron laughed, and Lord Lascher appeared unamused.

"Well you don't." She protested.

"It's the accomplishment—the knowledge you are the best." Lord Lascher's brow furrowed into a frown.

"Why not just tell yourself you're the best and spend your time making something real, instead?"

"That's just not how people or demons work."

A loud scream interrupted the conversation. They all turned to see a young man in a suit roar as he ran face first into a wall a few feet away from them. He bounced off the wall and flopped onto the floor. He appeared unconscious as he landed on his back near the water cooler.

"Is stupidity how they work?" Dora asked, watching a dopey smile spread across the young man's face.

"Well, yes. Stupidity is a main part of the human psyche." Lord Lascher admitted.

"What do *they* win?" Kieron grinned, pointing to a fornicating couple who were making out against the glass partition in the office behind Lord Lascher.

Dora stifled a shocked laugh. They were really going for it. Their clothes were hanging off them, and their hands were twisted up in the venetian blinds. They appeared oblivious to the audience they had on the other side of the glass.

"We like to let office relationships develop to a point. However, this kind of relationship should be an office secret." Lord Lascher's eyes widened as the girl's naked ass cheeks slammed against the glass.

"Why does it need to be a secret?" Kieron asked.

"So people don't see naked ass in their faces," Dora

muttered as the ass cheeks slapped against the glass again and spread across it.

"No, it's just more exciting if you're not allowed to do it. We make sure our office workers all fear being caught doing it. It makes the office romances more exciting for them," Lord Lascher said.

"They seem pretty excited without the secrets." Dora commented, watching the naked, entwined bodies ferociously maul each other.

"Yes they do, don't they? Still, it's against company policy. They'll get fired for it." Lord Lascher appeared saddened as he shook his head.

A plump woman, wearing a gray jumpsuit, stormed into the office containing the copulating couple. Her tight bun of dark hair pulled against the skin on her face, stretching her harsh features. She carried a clipboard in one hand and a nozzle style gun in the other. She had a large canister strapped to her back, which Dora realized attached to the nozzle as the woman turned to close the door behind her.

The couple were still going crazy over each other and using far too much tongue in Dora's opinion. "Who's she? A Ghostbuste—" Dora didn't finish her sentence as the lady said something unintelligible to the couple and pointed the nozzle of her tank at them. The couple didn't react or even notice she was there. After a few seconds, she fired. Flames blazed out of the nozzle and doused the couple in fire, burning them to a crisp in a few short seconds.

"That's HR," Lord Lascher said, guiding Dora and

Kieron to face the opposite direction. Dora was thankful to look away from the charred corpse butt on the window and across the open plan office instead. "Whatever you two do, don't mess with HR." Lord Lascher warned.

# 21

# SKY HUNTRESS

Dora glanced at Kieron. He was almost bouncing up and down with excitement at the prospect of visiting the Punishment Sector today. She peered around Lord Lascher's office in Corporate Hell, feeling bored. *If today involves filing again, I'm so outta here.*

She noticed a small bulge moving inside her backpack and bent over the table to be closer to it. "Stop wriggling so much, Pooey," she whispered.

"My ass has gone numb." Pooey complained.

"Well, rub it."

"Great, just what I always wanted, to rub my *own* ass better." Pooey grumbled.

"What?" Kieron peered at Dora.

"Oh, I was just talking to myself." Dora sat up straight and attempted to appear innocent.

"Ohh, okay. Do you do that often?" He studied her from a safe distance.

"Yes, I'm totally crazy. I also check my palms

regularly for hairs growing on them," she replied, rolling her eyes.

"Why wouldn't you?" Kieron glanced down at his own palms and studied them. "I can't wait until mine grow in."

Dora blinked at him. *Is he being serious?*

"Okay kids. Are you ready for some fun?" Lord Lascher burst into the office. Dora nearly fell off her chair at the sound of his booming voice.

"Hell yes!" Kieron was already out of his seat and standing beside his father.

"Can't wait." Dora grimaced, imagining a day of mundane office work ahead. She stood up and grabbed her bag off the table. When she swung it over her shoulder, she coughed to cover up the muffled protests coming from Pooey.

"This way." Lord Lascher guided them out of the office. They followed him down a long, dark corridor, which appeared to go on forever. A pinch of fear made her pause as the idea of being stuck in the office forever invaded her thoughts. She sighed and continued when an escalator came into view ahead. She thanked all that was unholy for an escape route as they went up the escalator. At the top, she noticed a chill in the air. It was the first time she'd ever felt cold in Hell.

They entered a large room, which looked like an airport check-in area. A line of counters faced them. Food stands were dotted near the exits and several doors led off to other rooms. The area was deserted. The hollow sound of their footsteps echoed around the room as they crossed the tiled floor, heading in the direction of a door marked 'Observation Deck'.

"This is so cool," Kieron whispered. He had a bright gleam of excitement in his eyes and a wide grin on his face.

Dora glanced at him as if he were crazy. "It's just an airport."

"No, it's so much more. You'll see."

She shrugged and found herself checking out Kieron's muscled back as he turned and headed towards the door. She dawdled behind him, not looking forward to the Punishment Sector at all. She couldn't be assed with another day at the office. Having her head cut off in school was more fun than this week in Corporate Hell had been.

*I thought evil was supposed to be exciting. What are we going to be learning about today? Evil vending machines and how to fill them up, evil databases and how to input data into them? No wait, I learnt that yesterday …*

Dora yawned as she followed Kieron and his father through the 'Observation Deck' doorway. *Everything here is so borin*—her brain froze as she stepped out on to a vast platform and looked around. There was no ceiling, only red swirling skies above her and no walls, just a low barrier around the edges. The barren landscape of Hell spread out behind the barrier. Her eyes widened as she saw her first view of Hell's wilderness, but it wasn't the vast stretch of red desert that made her jaw drop open in shock. Directly ahead of her were rows upon rows of sleeping dragons, in varying shades. Massive beasts with fangs the size of Dora were curled up in football-field sized enclosures. Some were sleeping and others were walking around the platform.

She stared in awe as a red scaly beast flew in from the sky and landed with an ear-shattering roar on a dusty runway.

"Aren't they beautiful?" Kieron asked, his eyes bouncing from the azure dragon to the emerald green one.

"Where did they come from?" she asked, unable to keep the awe from her voice as she watched the red dragon walk to an empty enclosure. She gasped when she noticed a rider on its back. The rider was tiny. A dot seated on the scaled back of a gigantic dragon.

"Long story, but you know about dinosaurs, right?" Kieron said.

"Prehistoric creatures, sure."

"Well, when they died ... er, some of them had been bad."

"Are you trying to tell me that dragons are dinosaurs in demon form?"

"Kinda."

"What do you mean?"

"Well, no one knows for sure because they keep their souls."

"Like me." Dora smiled. She liked the idea of being similar to one of these majestic beasts.

"But they're dead, we think ..."

"You don't know?"

"Would you want to poke one to find out?"

"Fair point," she said. "Who's she?" She pointed to the leather-clad pilot of the red dragon as she jumped down off the massive red beast and patted it on the snout.

"Oh, that's the Sky Huntress," he replied.

"Who's she?"

"She's like the general for the air force here. The dragons have always let her fly them. No one knows why.

Dora watched Lord Lascher approach the Sky Huntress. She wore flying goggles, so Dora couldn't see much of her face. Her long blond hair flew behind her as a gust of wind blew across the platform. Her leather suit clung to her shapely figure. She wore a lethal-looking steel gauntlet on her left arm and carried a whip in her other hand.

Lord Lascher said something to her, and she shook her head. He said something else, which must have angered her because she uncurled her whip and let it trail on the floor as if preparing to strike him. He backed away from her, shaking his head and holding his hands in front of him.

"What's he doing?" Dora asked.

"Probably making an ass of himself," Kieron replied.

Lord Lascher appeared to be speaking quickly to the Sky Huntress. Whatever he said must have worked because her posture relaxed, and the whip remained at her side. Dora tried to listen to the conversation, but the whoosh of air over the platform distorted all the sounds around her.

She shrugged and glanced upwards, gazing in awe at

the hundreds of dragons in the sky above her. Their massive wings flapped over the platform as they twirled and darted in the air. Each dragon had a rider seated in the golden saddles on their backs. She realized they were coordinated as they swooped through the air in formation. "Oh, wow," she muttered, staring up at the team of airborne dragons.

Kieron glanced up too. "Amazing, aren't they?"

"Are those all sky er, hunters?" she asked, pointing to the riders.

"No, there's only one Sky Huntress. Those are her flyers. They're all under her command. See that one there, on the silver dragon?"

Dora searched the skies for a silver dragon. She could just make out the dark-haired rider on its back.

"That's PattiAvilla, the second-in-command. Dad got me her autograph once," he said with excitement in his voice.

"Screw an autograph. I want to ride her dragon!"

Kieron laughed. "I doubt they'll let us. They won't even let dad ride one. Well, he tried once and nearly lost his head, literally."

"Won't it just grow back though? He is a demon, right?"

"Funny thing about dragons; if one kills you in Hell, you kinda stay dead."

"How is that even possible?"

He shrugged. "No one knows. Dragons are mysterious creatures even to us."

"Okay. That was hard work, but we're in." Lord

Lascher shouted over the noise of flapping of wings as he returned to Dora and Kieron.

"In what?" Kieron asked.

"The Sky Huntress has allowed us to join her on her next mission."

"Whoa! Are you for real?" Kieron squealed like an excited teenage girl at a Bieber concert.

"You just lost two thousand man points with that squeal." Dora told Kieron.

"Bite me! I get to fly a dragon," he replied in a slightly deeper voice.

"What is the mission, anyway?" She turned to ask Lord Lascher.

"We get to hunt down runaway narcissists." Lord Lascher also sounded like an excited teenage girl.

"If you two don't calm down, I'm going to start braiding your hair." She told both the Laschers.

"Well said." The Sky Huntress's voice was sultry and commanding at the same time. Dora jumped when she heard it coming from behind her. She turned to face the pilot who stood a few feet away.

"Shall we?" The Sky Huntress gestured towards her red dragon, inviting them to climb aboard.

Dora eyed the flimsy belt around her waist. It was supposed to strap her to the saddle on the back of the dragon. She glanced sideways at Kieron, who was staring in awe at the red dragon scales beneath his feet.

"Psst! Is this safe?" she hissed at Kieron.

"What? Oh yeah, worst case scenario, you fall out," he replied while gazing around in awe.

"Won't I die if I fall out?"

"Why the fuck can I smell dragon?" Pooey's voice burst out of Dora's backpack.

"Is that Pooey?" Kieron spun around in his seat with surprise widening his eyes.

"What?" She attempted to appear innocent. The sound of whooshing wings and dragon growls drowned out Kieron's reply as the red wings of the dragon flapped, and the giant beast bounded down the runway with them strapped to its back.

"Oh fuck. I'm gonna barf!" Pooey yelped.

Kieron gripped her hand as if suddenly realizing she was only human. Her ears popped as the muscles in the massive beast shifted beneath them. A harsh gust of wind pushed them back in their seats as they launched into the air.

"Ye haaaa! Lord Lascher shouted from the passenger seat in front of them, thrusting his fist into the air in triumph as they took off. He sat beside the Sky Huntress, who shook her head at him. Dora watched the Sky Huntress's hair catch the wind in golden tendrils. She appeared at ease in the sky, seated on the back of the giant dragon.

After the horrifying takeoff, Dora relaxed a little. The ride settled down to a smooth flight as it passed over the barren landscape of Hell.

"Did I hear Pooey?" Kieron demanded.

"You might have," she replied, hugging her backpack.

"You shouldn't take him out of the house. He might get lost."

"He was scared he'd be eaten by *your* mother. I couldn't leave him behind."

"He's luncheon meat to anyone in Corporate Hell. Keep him out of sight," Kieron whispered.

"But he's too cute to eat."

"Bite me." Pooey's voice came from within the backpack.

"He should know better than to leave the safety of Castle Lascher," Kieron said to the backpack. "I'm surprised he hasn't been eaten by someone before now."

"I. R. Ninja," Pooey replied, slowly pronouncing each word.

"U. R. A. Pain in the a—"

Dora punched Kieron in the arm before he could finish. "Dragon ride now. Bitch fight later," she said to them both.

"Target up ahead." The Sky Huntress called out over the sound of dragon wings flapping. She pointed to a figure running away in the distance.

Dora stared at the tiny man below them. He ran away from the approaching dragon and screamed. The dragon swooped down towards him. He glanced back at them and shrieked, scrambling over sharp cliffs in an attempt to escape.

"What did he do wrong?" Dora shouted to Lord Lascher.

Lord Lascher turned back towards her. "He thought the world owed him a favor," he shouted in reply.

"Is that such a big sin?" she asked.

"It is when you sell your own daughter to the Russian Mafia, so you can live on easy street."

She shook her head in disgust. *What a scumbag.*

"How do you think we should punish him, Dora?" Lord Lascher had a wicked gleam in his eyes.

"Have this dragon burn him alive."

"No can do." The Sky Huntress called out. "I didn't have time to refuel."

Lord Lascher sighed. "What can we do?"

"Bite him," the Sky Huntress replied.

Dora grinned as an idea popped into her head. "How big is dragon poop?"

The Sky Huntress turned back to face Dora and flashed a smile at her. Her golden eyes twinkled with amusement. "Big enough," she replied.

The dragon zeroed in on the man and glided over him with stretched out wings.

"Bombs away!" The Sky Huntress commanded.

Dora stared down at the man and giggled when he looked into the sky at the worst possible moment. His eyes widened in horror as tons of steaming dragon shit fell towards him. He held up his hands in an attempt to protect himself against an avalanche of shit, but even Dora could tell it wasn't going to do him any good.

Green and brown colored, steaming dragon excrement splattered a fifty-foot radius around the man, drowning him in dragon crap and flattening him in an instant.

"You have an attraction to shit, don't you?" Kieron asked before bursting out laughing.

Dora shot Kieron a sideways glance. She had to bite the inside of her cheek to refrain from commenting.

# 22
## MENACING MACHINATIONS

"I need to visit the rest room. I'll be back in a minute," Kieron said as he left Dora standing at the entrance of the Burning Rock Café. She surveyed the restaurant. It was a thriving cafe with a mixture of demons milling around inside. Fire shot up the walls in random bursts, illuminating and decorating the room. The main seating area was home to round leather booths with large black tables inside them.

*I hope they don't serve dragon in here, or it'll ruin the perfect day.* After a fantastic day riding dragons, Lord Lascher had promised to treat her and Kieron to a great meal on the way home. So far, it'd been the best day ever for Dora.

"Let's get a table," Lord Lascher said before he led her through the busy American-style restaurant and towards one of the red leather booths. She eyed the Flamin' Grill as she passed it. Her stomach flipped over, and she felt queasy when she looked at the rump steak. It was a grilled butt, made of actual butt cheeks. *Please let them sell something ordinary like fries here.*

Lord Lascher chose a table at the back. She stifled a giggle as she watched him attempt to slide into the booth with some dignity, which was physically impossible. He ended up looking harassed by the seating with his debonair black suit twisted around him and crumpled up.

She stepped back for a better view, biting back the urge to laugh. Her laugh escaped with a loud 'Ha' when someone knocked into her. She spun around to see a waiflike waitress losing her balance behind her. The waitress held a mountain of cutlery, precariously balanced in a plastic tub on her left arm. The cutlery spilled as she wobbled, and a few spoons toppled over the edge of the tub and clattered to the floor with loud clinks.

Dora reached out a hand to steady the demon, but too late. The tub flipped over and fell, dropping an avalanche of silver implements on the floor. The waitress groaned before sinking to her knees and gathering up the forks and knives off the floor.

She was a tiny, little thing with short red hair and catlike green eyes. Dora sank to her knees beside her and helped her pick up the silver spoons and fallen forks. "Sorry," Dora mumbled, feeling guilty for knocking into her. "I should have watched where I was going."

"It's okay. Thanks for the help." The waitress peered up at her with a sweet smile. Her eyes glowed with a hazy green light. For a moment, all Dora could see were the waitress's eyes. She felt a strange tug inside her chest. She shook her head to try to clear the woozy feeling. A wave of dizziness washed over her when she handed the waitress the collection of cutlery she'd collected for her.

Dora frowned when it took all her concentration to stand back up as she forced herself to rise from her kneeling position. She shook her head and blinked several times. *Ooh, dizzy.*

She turned away from the waitress and slumped into her seat in the booth opposite Lord Lascher to stop herself from falling over or fainting. She tried to clear her mind and focused on Lord Lascher instead. He was frowning at her with a dark look in his eyes.

Without warning, he pointed his arm at the waitress as she scurried towards the doors. "Incinerato," he cried. A ball of fire shot from his fingers. Dora watched it shoot across the room of astonished diners and explode when it hit the waitress in the center of her back. She burst into flames, screaming as the fire devoured her.

She spun around to face her attacker as her body burst into flames. Her green eyes shone, and her sharp fangs sprang out over her bottom lip. Her pink skin transformed into green scales before she exploded into a ball of writhing fire. She blackened to a charred husk as the flames died out, and her carcass crumbled to the floor in a pile of ashes.

"What the fu—" Dora began.

Lord Lascher silenced her by holding a tiny white crystal in front of her face. "Do you know what this is?"

"Um, a soul-chip."

"Not just any soul-chip. This one is yours. It's just been chipped off your soul."

"How did you get it?" Dora snapped. She curbed the urge to stab him through the face with a fork. Not only had he killed the waitress, he'd stolen a piece of Dora's soul too.

"By level law, upon death all property of the deceased reverts to the demon that killed them." Lord Lascher rolled the soul-chip across his palm.

Dora stared at the chip. It was nearly pure white with only a hint of something darker tainting it. "Wait, so ..."

"So I killed the waitress for stealing a piece of your soul—to get it back. And *that* was no waitress." Lord Lascher's black eyes swirled with anger.

"What was she?" Dora glanced at the smoking pile of ash, feeling queasy.

"She was an arkeol demon. They're treasure hunters by nature, often found following shiny things in their natural habitat. Although in recent times they've traveled into the larger cities where their abilities to find things of value is put to less innocent uses."

"Such as?" she asked.

"Oh, you know, sucking the souls out of innocent girls, grave robbery, working for the Dark Auctions, being resellers on Amazon—that kind of thing," Lord Lasher replied. "Judging by her markings, she worked for the Dark Auctions, which means she didn't pick you at random. Someone knows you have a soul. There must have been a request for it at the auction house. If you'd let her, she'd have drained it all out of you, a piece at a time." Lord Lascher dropped the soul-chip in his breast pocket and shook his head. "Dora, we need to make you evil faster. You're not safe until you can defend yourself. You're not safe when you're being nice to every demon that plays with your stupid human emotions."

Dora scowled at Lord Lascher. She was pissed off, mainly because he was right. Mostly, she was angry with herself for being so gullible. *The waitress must have knocked into me on purpose to get my sympathy. Is that how they take your soul, by playing on your sympathy?* She realized she needed to start acting like a demon, or she'd never survive in Hell. Dark thoughts plagued her mind as she stood up. In a fit of rage, she walked over to the pile of dust and kicked it, sending clouds of demon ash across the white tiled floor.

"Did someone burn your dinner?" Dora turned to encounter Kieron's innocent eyes when he appeared behind her.

"Something like that," she muttered in a dark voice.

"Aww, don't worry we'll get you something else," he said with a smile.

She scowled at the black ash on the floor. "That won't be necessary. I'll fix it myself." She glanced at Lord Lascher. He nodded with a glint of approval in his dark eyes.

*This time, I'm really going to embrace evil.*

"What the fuck are you doing?" Pooey asked.

"I'm revising." Dora put down the book and glanced at her furry friend.

Pooey inclined his head sideways and read the book title. "In a book about vegetables?" He didn't appear convinced.

"No, this is …" She read the title and winced. *'Opscurum vegetus' means dark magic, doesn't it?*

"Dark vegetables," he said. "What? Are you studying the menacing machinations of a potato?"

"Shit!" She dropped the book and scowled at it. "How am I supposed to learn evil when I can't even read the book title?"

"Why do you wanna be evil?" Pooey scratched his chin while studying her.

"So I can defend myself in Hell and stay here."

"Really?" He raised a skeptical eyebrow.

"Yes, why else?"

"Oh, I dunno … power, greed and world domination. Things like that."

"I er, what do you know about world domination?"

"That it's never as easy as people say it will be." Pooey complained. "Anyway, you don't need a book to be evil. You just need to care more about yourself than anyone else. That *always* works."

"Be selfish?" Dora didn't like the idea.

"The idea feels dirty doesn't it? Yep, that's when you know you're being bad. The trick is learning to ignore the guilt. Why do you need to learn evil so fast, anyway? It's ages until the big test."

"It's the mock exams in the dining room today at …" Dora glanced at the clock. "Crap, now!" She jumped out of her chair and dashed for the doorway, glancing back for a second at Pooey. "Thanks," she said.

"Not selfish enough." He commented.

"Fine. Fuck off." She winked at his pouting, furry face before racing downstairs.

## 23

## DEMONS OF THE ARENA

Kieron pulled a number two pencil out of his bag and placed it on the desk in front of him in preparation for the mock exam. He was nervous, but not about the exam. The knot in his stomach was about the idea of going head-to-head with Dora. She was bound to fail, and that would make her unhappy. All morning, he'd been trying to think of ways to let her win. But since his father hadn't given any hints about the subject of the exam, there were no answers to give her in advance. *Maybe she'll win. She has so far in Hell.*

However, he had done mock exams several times, and not once had it been easy. He knew even Dora couldn't horseshit her way out of this one.

He glanced at his father, who stood in silence near the whiteboard, polishing his glasses. They were both waiting for Dora to appear.

Kieron frowned. For Dora to stay here, she had to ace this exam, but it was complicated. To stay here, she also had to help him improve at being evil. His father had made it abundantly clear. The only reason Dora was here was to sort out his son.

He clenched his fist around the pencil as the dilemma gnawed at him. Should he try his best, or should he try his worst? Should he win this competition and show Dora to be a good influence? It would appease his parents and gain their support in helping Dora stay in Hell. The other option was to let her win, thus proving she could pass the exams.

Hell didn't give everyone a grade for competing. There was only one winner in these kinds of tests. They were competitions where the winners were rewarded, and the losers were made to suffer. *But, who should win it?*

Against his own instincts, Kieron knew Dora had to lose today. At the very least, he had to try his best. If he helped her win the mock exams, she'd never try hard enough on the real ones, and she needed to win those. *I hope I'm not matched against her on Judgment Day, or we're screwed!*

He peered at the clock. It was nearly time for the exam to start. *Where the hell is she?*

A loud crash echoed in the hallway. The door swung open, and Dora burst into the room. She was panting and holding onto the doorframe. Her red T-shirt hung off her dainty shoulder, baring her soft skin. Her hair bounced around her head in a wild tumble of dark curls. She inhaled a couple of slow breaths before pushing herself off the doorway and walking into the room. Kieron smiled, enjoying the view.

"Did I make it?" She gasped.

"Yes you did," his father replied. "But only just."

"Sorry." She rushed over to the desk beside Kieron and flashed him a smile. His heart did a little leap for joy. He had to fight to contain the guilt that followed it. *I'll try to make it quick and painless for you.* A feeling of sadness threatened to overwhelm him

"Now we're all here, we can begin." His father stood up and lifted a staff off the wall. The staff was a long copper pole with carvings of demigods and tortured souls running down the length of it. On top of the staff was a blood-red gem the size of a fist. Kieron recognized it. It was the Demon Gauntlet.

"Why do you have the De—" he began.

"Arentha!" His father banged the staff on the ground, cutting off his question. *Aww shit!*

The room spun, rapidly becoming a blur. Kieron held onto his desk as the walls smudged into white mush before his eyes. He jerked his head towards Dora to ensure she was okay and gasped when she slipped sideways in her seat. The room picked up speed and spun crazily out of control. He reached for her and grabbed her hand, so the cyclone wouldn't pull her away. The muscles in his arm bulged up, and his knuckles whitened from holding onto her with all his strength.

The force of the spinning made him shift in his chair. He glanced down and realized he was falling. The cyclone pushed them both to the edges of the room, so he hugged his desk with his free hand in an attempt to keep hold of something solid.

*What, in the name of all that is unholy, is this?* He had only read about the Demon Gauntlet in history books. He knew it was some kind of competition, but that was all he knew.

The cyclone ripped Dora's chair out from beneath her, and she let out a scream. He tightened his grip on her wrist when her desk crashed into the spinning walls of the room. The only thing keeping her from following it was his grip on her hand. His desk shifted under him as the pull of gravity tried to tug it outwards. The room became a rotating blur, an unrecognizable smudge surrounding them. An abyss appeared at the far edges of the cyclone, swirling around them.

Kieron tried to hold onto the desk, but he panicked when Dora's hand slipped out of his. He watched in horror as the cyclone pulled her away from him. He released his desk and gripped her arm with both of his hands, refusing to let her go. The desk dropped into the growing abyss below them, making him cry out in fear.

"Shit!" His stomach jumped into his mouth when he and Dora fell down into a black spinning tunnel with only each other's hands to hold onto.

They fell for only a short distance before hitting the ground with a loud thud.

His first sensation was sand in his face. He lifted his head and spat the dust out of his mouth, wondering where he was. He groaned and flexed his arms. He could still feel Dora's wrist encased in his fingers, so he peered sideways to find her. When he discovered her lying face down in the red sand beside him, he exhaled a sigh of relief.

He enjoyed the feel of solid earth beneath his body before lifting his head to speak. "Dora, are you okay?"

"What the fuck was that?" She sounded really pissed off and slightly muffled by the sand in her face.

"I don't know." He released her hand and rolled onto his back. He widened his eyes when he looked up to see an inky blanket of sky with a sprinkling of stars and two moons. "Where the hell are we?"

"Welcome to the Kikssa Arena!" His father's voice boomed at them in the distance.

Kieron sat up, scanning the arena to locate his father. A dark coliseum made of sharp twisted metal surrounded them, and they lay upon the red sands of Hell. *Is this a staging ground for battle?*

His father stood directly ahead of them on a podium that jutted out of the main coliseum like a stage. The podium connected to the empty stands encircling the arena.

He narrowed his eyes at his father. Not a hair on his obnoxious head was out of place. Holding the staff must have protected him from the journey here. *Twat!*

Dora rolled over and looked up. She rested on her elbows, raising her back off the ground. Kieron peered down at her slender form, taking a moment to enjoy the view of her body languidly sprawled out on the arena floor. *I wonder what she'd do if I kissed her right now.* His eyes traveled to her face. She was staring at his father and frowning. *She'd probably bite me for it.*

He wondered idly for a moment where she would bite him, and if he'd enjoy it before his father's voice broke the spell of Dora.

"To the death." His father bellowed, throwing two staves on the floor of the arena.

The staves landed near their feet, and Dora glanced at them with a blank expression on her face.

Kieron clenched his fists in anger. "Are you shitting me?" he shouted at his father.

"What are we supposed to do?" Dora asked. Although, judging by the look on her face, she had an idea of what was supposed to happen next.

"I'm not doing it." He folded his arms and looked away from his staff.

"What happens if we don—?" Dora began.

In reply to her question, deadly-looking metal spikes shot up through the ground around them, making both Kieron and Dora jump.

"To the death." His father repeated with finality in his tone.

"This is just bullshit," Kieron cried. "Fine. Whatever!" He turned to Dora. "Pick up a staff, and attack me with it. It's the only way."

"But I don't want to hurt yo—" More spikes shot up through the sands around them, and they were getting closer—too close.

He knew that if too many spikes popped up, they would impale him and Dora. "We don't have a choice." He jumped to his feet and pulled Dora onto hers. He reached down, grabbed one of the staves and put it in her hand. "Just kill me, and get it over with."

Dora frowned. She appeared upset by the suggestion.

"It won't hurt me. It's okay." He lied.

Dora examined the staff in her hand before glancing at him with confusion and fear in her eyes.

More spikes shot up through the earth, causing his pulse to race with fear. *If she doesn't do it soon, we'll both die.*

"Just fucking attack me, and stop messing around!" he shouted at her with panic bubbling in his chest. He'd come back from being killed, but Dora wouldn't.

A spark of anger lit up in her eyes, and they narrowed to slits. She raised the staff above him, flashing him a wicked glare. He froze in fear when she gave him a hard smack on the head with her staff.

Inky darkness swallowed him as he slipped into unconsciousness with one final thought filling his mind. *Crap! Doesn't she know staves are meant for spell casting?*

Dora watched Kieron crumple to the ground before glancing at the stick in her hand. *Why are we hitting each other with sticks?* She shrugged. *That was easy.*

"Okay you can turn off the spikes now. I won," she shouted to Lord Lascher. She couldn't understand why Lord Lascher had his head in his hands, or why he was shaking his head so much.

"What? I bonked him with the stick. Did I pass?"

"You were supposed to kill him!" Lord Lascher screamed at her.

"With a stick? Gimme a bazooka next time if you

want to see blood spatter." She knelt over Kieron, brushing sand off his cheek. She was relieved to find him snoring like a baby and unharmed by her attack.

"It's a *staff,* you idiot!" Lord Lascher shouted back.

Dora scowled and stood up. She faced Lord Lascher and growled. *No one calls me an idiot.* She angrily waved the stick at him. "Screw you!" she screamed.

Lord Lascher's face paled. She watched in awe as he spun around on the spot, slowly at first then faster and faster. He shrank as if being screwed into the ground, but he didn't make a dent in the steel platform he stood upon. His body squashed downwards instead, every time it turned.

She gulped, and her stomach turned when Lord Lascher's body bulged as his bones crunched downwards into places they shouldn't go. His skin stretched as if it were about to pop under the pressure of being screwed down.

She turned away to see Kieron sitting up beside her. She glanced down at him, horrified. "I-I didn't mean to—" she stammered.

A loud groaning sound caused her to spin around to face the platform, just as Lord Lascher's body popped like a grape in a vice and splattered all over the podium.

"Just be thankful you didn't shout, 'fuck you asshole' while holding that thing." Kieron nodded at the staff, laughing. "He's going to be pissed when he comes back."

Dora gulped. She'd just squished her teacher. She'd just killed someone! There was a sickening sensation in her stomach telling her it was very wrong to kill Lord

Lascher, but the weapon in her hand made her feel powerful. She glanced down at the staff. "Are we allowed to keep these?"

# SPAZMERELDA

K ieron faced a tentacled beast with only a feather duster in his hands for a weapon. He glanced at the pink fluffy weapon with disbelief. *What the fu—*

The beast knocked the duster out of his hand with one of its meaty red tentacles and slapped him across the face with another at the same time.

He hunkered down low to avoid another vicious swipe from it. His heart hammered, and beads of sweat rolled down his forehead. He stared at the wicked green eyes of the creature. Its abnormally small head followed his every move as its waving tentacles surrounded it. It didn't have a body, just arms attached to a pea head. *Its head must be its weak spot,* he realized. *It's now or never.*

He ran at the monster, letting out a loud roar and launching himself at it. Slimy tentacles wrapped around him, squeezing his chest and making it impossible for him to breathe. He struggled and tried to cry out. But when he opened his mouth, no sound came out. The tentacles tightened. He gasped, feeling as if his insides were about to explode. *I'm going to die!*

He slammed onto the floor as he rolled off his bed and landed in a heap. Wrapped up in the tangled maze of his bed sheet, he struggled to get out of it. It took a moment for him to realize he'd been asleep, and the tentacled monster had been his bed sheet.

Kieron groaned and wriggled to escape the confining bed sheet. Something was terribly wrong. *Demons don't dream!*

With his muscles still trembling with adrenaline, he cautiously peered around his bedroom. The large mahogany closet still stood in the corner of the room next to a matching desk and a few bookshelves. His brown-leather La-Z-Boy armchair was still at the end of his bed, opposite his X-box 360. Next to the chair was the mini-fridge that he used to cool his cans of Red Bull. Even though his most precious items were all accounted for, he couldn't shake the nagging feeling that something was wrong.

He struggled out of the last tendril of sheet and stood up. His bedroom door caught his eye as it shimmered with a purple haze. He rubbed his eyes to ensure it wasn't just him and looked again. A faint purple mist shimmered in front of the doorway.

Kieron stepped closer to the fog and stretched out his hand to touch it. A red tentacle came out of the haze and slapped him across the face. He jumped back with a yelp. Something was stopping him from leaving the room. He searched the room for a weapon. His eyes fell upon a pink feather duster, which Maisie the maid-demon must have left on his bedside table. *Oh, come on. You've gotta be kidding me! What is this, Groundhog Day?*

It was as if the dream had been a warning of what was to come, but he never dreamed. Was it a warning? Why would he dream now? *Okay, I need to be clever about this. Running for the door isn't going to work.*

He glanced out of the window at the street below and contemplated trying to climb down the side of the castle, but the castle was made of smooth onyx with several sharp spires and ledges for him to become impaled on.

*D'ho, Magic. I'll just use magic.* He stared at the door, frowning with concentration as he tried to cast a spell on it. "Releashio," he muttered. Nothing appeared to have changed, but he reached a hand into the purple haze again anyway. An angry red tentacle slapped his hand away.

"Damn it." He tried the spell again, this time forcing all his senses to concentrate on the door. "RELEASHIO!"

The red tentacle waved out of the purple mist and waggled at him in a disapproving manner.

"Son of a bitch!" He snapped at it, trying to grab it. The feeler waved out of his way and bitch-slapped him across the left cheek several times instead before eventually knocking him backwards onto his ass.

Kieron landed on the hard wooden floor with a groan. *What the hell is this? Has it attacked the whole castle? Is Dora okay?* Panic and fear over what may be happening to Dora forced him to react with a sense of urgency. He ran at the door with no thought for his own safety and slammed into a wall of purple mist. He growled and pushed it back an inch at a time, fighting his way through it with determination and straining his demon muscles.

The haze weakened. After pushing against it, snarling and growling, he eventually burst through the doorway. He smashed into the oak panels, ripping the door off its hinges and tumbling into the corridor outside of his room. He nearly stumbled over the balustrade in the process. Using all his strength to stop himself before he took a nasty spill over the railing, he gripped the banister, pushing back against it. He spun around in preparation to fight the monstrous red beast blocking his door.

He blinked. *Where is it?*

He studied his bedroom door. It was now hanging off its frame in splintered pieces. The purple haze had evaporated, and there was nothing there.

Kieron frowned when he heard a small squeak coming from somewhere near the door. He leaned over the wreckage. The sound emanated from beneath a broken piece of wood, which gently wobbled. Sticking out from under the wood was a pair of tiny female legs.

He lifted the wood and stared down at the miniature blond-haired woman lying on the floor. She wore a purple princess dress and a tiny silver tiara. She sparkled everywhere except her feet, which were encased in black biker boots. She had little, transparent wings and long, pointy ears, one of which was bent at an awkward angle.

"Don't hurt me!" She squeaked. "I was only doing my job."

"Your job?" Kieron scowled as she waved her hands in a placating gesture, and purple dust fell from them. "What exactly is *your job*?"

"I was paid to keep you inside your room," she said. "I'm innocent, I swear."

"Who paid you?"

"I can't go divulging my clients. It'd ruin my reputation."

"Your reputation as what? What the hell are you?"

"Can't you tell?" She stood up before flying up towards his face and hovering in front of him. She stuck her ass and chest out at the same time in a dainty pose, batting her pretty eyelashes at him.

Kieron slapped himself in the forehead when he realized what she was. "You're a fucking fairy, aren't you?"

"Dark fairy—it's dark fairy, not fucking fairy!" She screeched at him, putting her tiny hands on her tiny hips.

"It's squashed fucking fairy if you don't tell me who hired you." Kieron snapped at her.

"Fine! It's not as if I'm getting paid for this job since you got out of the room. Lord Lascher paid me to keep you in your room." Her eyes narrowed as she studied him. "What are you anyway? No demon should have been able to get through my blockade." She looked him up and down. "Half breed?"

"I am *not* a bloody half breed!" Kieron wanted to strangle her. Why did demons always assume there was something wrong with him? He was just a bit too nice. That was all.

"Well, whatever. I didn't sign up to babysit someone like *you*, so I'll be on my way."

"Babysit? You trapped me in my room with a big red monster!"

"Meh, semantics," she muttered.

"Why did my father want me trapped in my room?" Kieron had a sinking suspicion it couldn't have been for anything good.

"I dunno, something about a door." The fairy shrugged, absentmindedly using her magic wand as a toothpick. "Can I go now? I've got a gig on DisneyLevel in an hour."

"A door? Wait—Dora. Do you mean Dora?" Kieron's pulse raced in panic. *What's he doing to her?*

"Yeah, that was it, a Dora. What is 'a Dora' anyway? And dude, you've gone as white as a sheet. Maybe you're half ghost?"

"I'm not half ghost." Kieron waved the question away as his mind ran over the possibilities. Dora had killed his father. Would his father do the same to her? He paced the hall worrying before pausing to glare at the fairy. "Dora is a name of a person. You do know what a name is, don't you?"

"Of course, I have a lovely name," the fairy said.

"What is it?"

"Spazmerelda," she said, puffing out her chest in pride.

He was lost for words over how awful her name was,

but decided it was best not to mention it to her. He found it difficult hold in a snigger, but she didn't notice.

"Can I go now? I've have thousands of whining demon spawn waiting to see me dance at the Fairy Godmother's Ball."

"Oh, that sounds nice."

"Yeah, we cut off a horse's head at the end. It's very dramatic."

"Eww." He wrinkled his nose in disgusted.

"You clearly have no concept of art." Spazmerelda huffed before she flew away muttering about critics.

Kieron shook his head as he watched Spazmerelda depart. *Fucking fairies.* He turned away as worry over Dora consumed his thoughts. He dashed down the hallway to her room and burst through the doorway.

"Dora, are you okay?" he cried.

She wasn't in her room, but it wasn't empty either. Slouched on her bed with a large tub of Ben and Jerry's, and surrounded by an array of snacks was a depressed-looking Pooey. Kieron stared at Pooey as he dipped his hand into a bag of cheesy puffs. He pulled out a handful of them before stuffing them into his mouth.

"Pooey, where's Dora? I think she's in trouble," Kieron said.

"Whash?" A spray of munched up cheesy puffs shot out of Pooey's full mouth and over Dora's bed.

"Eww, don't speak with your mouth full," Kieron muttered.

"Thash right!" Pooey sprayed another blast of cheesy puffs onto the bed before swallowing the remaining snacks in his mouth. "That's right. Pick on Pooey. Pooey does everything wrong. Pooey sucks. Pooey sucks so bad he got named *Pooey*!" The little, brown fluffy demon shrieked before slamming his fist in the bag of cheesy puffs and grinding them into crumbs in the process.

"I er, never said you sucked."

"Go away," Pooey muttered as he licked an ice cream spoon and sadly stared down at his protruding, fluffy belly.

Kieron felt a moment of sympathy for the little guy. *What happened to him?* "Are you okay?" he asked, taking a seat beside him on the edge of the bed. He frowned. Pooey never acted this depressed. Something must have happened.

His sympathy for the little demon evaporated when Pooey burped with a loud 'warp' noise that echoed through the room. "Aww, come on. That's just gross."

"Bite me," Pooey replied, stuffing a whole cookie into his mouth.

"Don't tempt me," Kieron muttered. "This is getting us nowhere. Have you seen Dora? Do you know where she is?"

Pooey nodded, and he gazed up at Kieron with big sad eyes that brimmed with helplessness.

"Is she okay? Did something happen?" As his worry increased, his stomach twisted into a knot of anxiety.

Pooey's cute and helpless eyes transformed into an evil glare when he narrowed them. "Is *she* alright? Ha! As if I care." Pooey rubbed his fluffy chin, and a few crumbs fell out of it into the tub of ice cream.

182

"Why wouldn't you? You like Dora," Kieron said, unsure of what he'd walked into.

"Used to. Don't like new Dora," Pooey mumbled. "She's mean."

"Dora's not mean." He smiled at Pooey to reassure him.

"Oh, yeah? So why did she steal my ninja skills and leave with your father while laughing at me?"

"What?"

"I was all happy and trusting with her. Stupid Pooey, I should have known better. This morning, in walks your father with a new spell for Dora. She needed my help, so I helped her. I didn't know the spell, but I trusted *her*. Next thing you know, she's waltzing off to a bar with your dad, and I'm stuck in here unable to leave. I tried every ninja trick I know, and all I can manage to do is summon a fat guy's lost weekend into the room." Pooey gestured to the array of snacks and candy on the bed. "I should have known better. Nobody loves Pooey." With his last sentence, Pooey dropped his head face first into the ice cream with a defeated sigh.

A muffled sound came from within the ice cream tub. Kieron gripped on the back of Pooey's shaggy head and pulled it out of the tub to discover he was still mumbling. "… and now I'm fat, and no one will ever love me …" He released Pooey's head, and his face dropped back into the ice cream with a plopping sound.

Dora had left with his father. Okay, that was somewhat understandable, but why would she take Pooey's ninja skills, and why had he been trapped in his room? He couldn't believe Dora would ever harm Pooey in any way, so there must be another explanation.

"Ohh!" He realized what had happened.

Pooey raised a curious, ice-cream-covered face out of the tub and eyed Kieron. "What?"

"I don't think she took your ninja skills. I was trapped in my room this morning too by my father and a fucking fairy."

"It's DARK FAIRY!" A small female voice screamed from the hallway.

Kieron spun around to see the angry little being fly into the room. Her face was red, and her hands were resting on her hips.

"I thought you had to go?" Kieron said.

Spazmerelda held her hands at either side of her, imitating a weighing scale. "Whining demon spawn or babysitting idiots. It's a tough choice."

"Did you take Pooey's ninja skills?" Kieron scowled at her.

Pooey's eyes narrowed to slits as he glared at the fairy.

"Take? No, I don't take. I hide," Spazmerelda said while studying her nails with wide, innocent eyes.

"Give me back my skills, hot fairy bitch." Pooey jumped to his feet and angrily brushed cookies and cream off his face.

"Do you really think I'm hot?" she asked.

"Graaaargh!" Pooey launched himself off the bed and into the air, grabbing Spazmerelda and landing on top of her with a loud thud. "Ninja skills, now! Or I warn you, it won't be pretty."

"Oh yeah, what are you gonna do?" She sniggered.

"Let's just say that after all the ice cream and given my sudden movement and my current position, you won't be pretty by the time I've finished with you." His stomach rumbled as if backing up his threat.

"Eww! Fine, whatever, have them back!" She clicked her fingers. A purple glow settled over Pooey, making him smile for a moment.

"Now let me go." Spazmerelda snapped, pushing at his fluffy shoulders with her tiny hands.

Pooey rolled off her and stood up with a happy shiver. His fur ruffled, and he grinned.

"Bloody demons." The fairy stood up, brushing her dress to smooth it down. She shot Pooey a sideways glance. "Do you really think I'm pretty, big fella?"

Kieron rolled his eyes when Pooey's chest puffed out at the words 'big fella'.

"Enough! Where the hell is Dora?" Kieron cried.

"She went for a drink with your dad," Spazmerelda said.

"Yeah, she did." Pooey confirmed.

"Did she go willingly?"

"Yeah, she was pretty happy," Spazmerelda said.

"She was giggling and didn't give a crap about me," Pooey added.

"Did she ask about me?" Kieron tried to understand why she would go without him.

"No." They replied in unison.

He slumped on the bed before picking up the tub of ice cream and the spoon. He looked into the tub. *It might make me feel better.*

"No!" he said, dropping the ice cream on the floor and standing up with renewed determination. "She would not have left me if she'd known I was trapped. It's my fucking father up to something again!"

"He is kinda sneaky." Spazmerelda agreed.

"He is a total dick," Pooey said.

"I'm going to get him back for this." Kieron narrowed his eyes and clenched his hands into fists.

# DEMON WARS

D ora woke up with a smile. She stretched out on her bed yawning. Last night had been amazing. She had learned about controlling demons while having a spa treatment from a coven of witches. Lord Lascher had told her it was an exploration into learning about her powers here in Hell. It had begun with therapy shopping at the most expensive boutiques and ended with a makeover at the Wych Spa. On top of all that, she could now control small demons with her willpower alone, which had been immense fun to learn. Although, when she tried it on Pooey last night, he'd just scowled at her and stomped away.

Dora frowned. *Why was Pooey so weird last night?* She sat up on the bed and scanned the room. "Pooey?"

The room was silent.

*Did something happen to him?* She began to worry. Pooey was always saying someone would eat him, but she had thought he'd be safe in her room.

"Pooey, where are you?" She jumped off the bed and searched the room for him. He wasn't under her bed or in her closet. She checked her backpack. He wasn't in there either. *Where the hell is he?*

Horrible thoughts of finding a half-eaten Pooey in the kitchen plagued Dora's mind as she frantically searched her room for the little ball of fluff.

When she couldn't find a hint of Pooey in the room, she decided to find Kieron. Maybe he could help. Not that he'd been particularly nice last night either, which had majorly pissed her off. He didn't appear to like her anymore. She'd tried asking Lord Lascher why Kieron hadn't come with them, but Lord Lascher had brushed the question away with a vague, 'Kieron won't be into all this girly stuff.' Nevertheless, she had felt abandoned by Kieron and assumed he had decided not to come with them because he didn't like hanging out with her anymore.

*Maybe he just wanted a break last night,* she rationalized, deciding to find Kieron and talk to him about it. He could help her find Pooey, and maybe they could bury any hatchets they had along the way.

Dora opened her bedroom door with a bright feeling of hope growing inside her. The feeling turned to ice before cracking into a million pieces and shattering when she saw Kieron leaving his room with Pooey sitting on his shoulder.

She stared at the backs of her *friends* as they walked down the corridor together, not even glancing in her direction. She silently closed her door and turned away from it when an overwhelming feeling of sadness washed over her. She sank against the door, sliding down it until she knelt on the plush red carpet in her bedroom. *I can't believe I worried about them, and they didn't even give me a second thought.*

Feelings of betrayal, sadness and anger overwhelmed her. She scowled, seeing red as the mindless urge to punch something exploded inside her. *How dare they ditch me?* She growled as she rose to her feet, and the anger built up inside her. A ball of fury grew in her belly, needing some kind of outlet.

She shrieked and spread her hands out towards her window. Fireballs shot from her fingertips, exploding on the window frame and engulfing the curtains. A feeling of emptiness washed over her as she stood there panting and watching the flames lick the curtains. The fire grew as it burned up into a blaze. She walked towards the window, feeling the heat of the fire warm her face. Her mind was blank as she watched the fire destroy the window frame, and the flames grow larger.

"Chill," she said in a dead tone. Ice formed on the window and doused the flames, creating a shiny coating over the burnt wood. She stared at it for a long time.

Eventually she frowned. *What the fuck was that?* She shook her head, feeling unsure about what had just happened, but she was more concerned by her sudden loss of allies than her curtain destroying skills. *What am I going to do if I have no friends here anymore?*

*Kill anything that gets in your way.* A dark voice in her mind replied.

Dora frowned. Even her thoughts were darker in Hell.

"Do you even know what you're doing?" Pooey shot Kieron an uneasy glance.

Kieron hung snotroot around his father's bedroom door. He paused and peered down at the little demon. "Trust me," he said. "This will keep him in his room."

"It wouldn't keep me in a room," Pooey replied.

"Well, you're a ninja, and he isn't," Kieron said with a sigh. He didn't actually know if this would work, but he had to try something to keep his father away from Dora, didn't he?

"That stuff is kinda gross." Pooey gestured at the goopy strings of snotroot hanging around the doorframe.

Kieron rolled his eyes and continued spreading the green gooey gel around the wooden frame with his fingers. *Does this guy ever shut up?*

"Kinda stinks too," Pooey said.

Kieron contained a growl and continued spreading the snotroot around the entrance to his father's chambers.

"I don't think it's going to work," Pooey added.

Kieron spun around and pointed a finger at Pooey. A large gob of snotroot flew off his hand and splatted Pooey in the face. "Shhh!" he hissed. "He can't wake up until I've finished.

"*Eww!*" Pooey cried, trying to wipe the hanging trails of snot off his face.

"Shush," Kieron whispered when he heard noises of

movement inside his father's chambers.

"Get this stuff off me. It's gross! Oh, my eyes. My eyes are stinging. I've been snotted! Help me." Pooey rolled around on the floor, attempting to wipe his face off on the thick red carpet.

"What the hell is going on out there?" Kieron heard his father shout inside his room.

"Shit," he muttered. He snatched the grimoire off the floor and quickly flipped to the bookmarked page for the right spell.

"Dude, I think you messed it up." Pooey paused rubbing his face on the carpet and peered up at Kieron.

"Not yet, I haven't." He ground out, trying to suppress the urge to kick Pooey. "Spiritus snotirious, with root of the giant nostril, I bind thee." He rushed out the words as the door handle turned.

He jumped back, nearly crushing Pooey as the door cracked open.

His father stood in the doorway wearing red silk pajamas. He had a confused expression on his face. "What the hell are you doing outside my bedroom?"

Kieron exhaled a deep breath before bravely puffing out his chest. "Protecting Dora from *you*."

"What have you done this time? Devil's balls, but you're an idiot of a son sometimes," his father muttered, taking a step towards Kieron. Green veins lit up in the gloopy snotroot around the doorway, and a large blob of it landed on Lord Lascher's head. He glanced up, frowning. "Oh, you fucking idio—" He didn't finish as the snotroot expanded with an elastic twang across the doorway, covering Lord Lascher in a thick jelly-substance and freezing him in it.

"Ooh, effective!" Pooey said, rubbing his chin and studying the frozen Lord Lascher, who now looked like a giant booger. "Will it go crusty later?"

Kieron hadn't actually read into what else the spell did, but seeing his father struggling through a wall of thick snot was kinda cool. Lord Lascher shouted something at Kieron, but the mucus covering him muffled the sound. Judging by his father's expression, he wasn't saying anything particularly pleasant.

"That's what you get for messing with *my girl*," Kieron said to the snot-frozen figure.

He took an involuntary step backwards when his father's eyes burned red, and he noticed the murderous look in them. *Oh shit!*

His father's face twisted and turned black. Large fangs grew over his lips. His muscles bulged as he changed into his demon form, and his body grew in size. The slimy covering expanded around him as his massive, veiny wings sprouted from his back. The gooey cage stretched as its prisoner expanded inside it until it finally exploded, splattering Kieron and Pooey with giant blobs of snot.

Kieron fell backwards when a giant gob of goop whapped him in the face. He landed on the floor next to a drenched Pooey.

"This is the last time I let you choose the spell," Pooey muttered, waving his drenched, fluffy arms in an attempt to shake the slime off them.

Kieron grimaced as he peered up at his father. The

black demon shook the snot off its scaly body, spraying mucus all over him and Pooey in the process.

Lord Lascher stared down at Kieron with angry blood-colored eyes. "Your ass is mine now, boy." His threatening growl sent a shiver down Kieron's spine.

When he didn't reply, the demon narrowed its eyes before a wicked smile lit up his face. "And so is your girl."

He scowled at his father and expelled a guttural growl of his own as his inner demon bubbled to the surface. Anger burned in the back of his throat as he jumped to his feet, feeling his demon muscles popping up all over his body.

"Dude, he's way scarier than you are," Pooey said.

Kieron spun his head around to face Pooey. He snarled at him. Pooey held up his hands in surrender. "I'm just sayin'."

Kieron turned back to face his father, narrowing his eyes at the black beast and clenching his fists. "Stay away from Dora."

"What are you going to do about it if I don't?" His father taunted. "You can't save her. She's already mine."

Fuelled by pure rage, he launched himself at his father and attacked with a loud roar. "*You* can't have her!"

Dora let out a polite cough before placing the tiny porcelain teacup back in its saucer with a dainty clink. She felt like a clumsy giant near Lady Lascher's fragile tea service. "Thank you for the tea, Lady Lascher."

After deliberating, she'd decided she needed a female point of view about her explosion in her room. With Kieron and Pooey abandoning her and Lord Lascher being useless to talk to because he was so vague about everything, her only option had been to find Lady Lascher and ask her advice. At least Lady Lascher would tell her what she genuinely thought, even if it was via her bipolar inner demon.

"You're welcome, Dora. I must say, it's nice to see you've been learning to use your abilities." Lady Lascher smiled, but her words were a little on the frosty side.

"I can't thank your family enough for helping me fit in," Dora said, deciding to butter her up for the best chance of decent advice.

"No need to thank us, my dear. I'm told Kieron's chances of passing his exams this year are much improved since you've been here." Lady Lascher placed her teacup on the side table and offered her a piece of carrot cake.

She winced when she accepted the cake. She didn't dare eat it for fear of spilling it on the pristine floral couch. She considered Lady Lascher's words. "I don't think I've done much to help Kieron, yet."

"No, not yet, but you will." Lady Lascher smiled again.

Dora frowned. *What the hell is that supposed to mean?* "What do you me—?" She didn't finish her question as a loud crash resonated behind her. She spun around to see Kieron and his father burst through the wall in a tumble of demon claws and bulging muscles. The black mass of Lord Lascher's demon form dwarfed

Kieron's tanned skin as they struggled and clawed at each other in a flurry of fists.

"Holy shit!" Dora gasped.

"Don't swear, dear. It's vulgar," Lady Lascher said as she placed her teacup in its saucer.

Kieron screamed when his father clawed at his chest, leaving trails of blood down it and shredding his white shirt to pieces. He punched his father in the stomach, and the giant demon groaned.

Lord Lascher retaliated, grabbing Kieron by the throat and lifting him into the air by his neck. Kieron wriggled like a worm on a hook, gasping in his father's grip. He appeared helpless as the black demon held him several feet above the ground.

"I vow by Satan's nutsack, if you don't put my son down right now, you'll regret it!" Lady Lascher's voice was cold, calm and deadly.

"I will after I've bitten his fucking head off," Lord Lascher replied as he bared his sharp fangs at Kieron.

"*Do not* make me angry." Lady Lascher snarled at her husband.

"Aww, come on. The little shit needs discipline." The black demon whined.

"Then I will do it. Put him down, NOW!"

Lord Lascher hissed at Lady Lascher before dropping Kieron onto the Oriental rug.

Dora rushed to Kieron's side as he sank to his knees panting for air. She touched his shoulder with tentative hands, wincing at his damaged skin. Deep scratches ran down his muscular chest and on to his defined abs. His shirt was ripped and hanging off him, and there were painful-looking red marks around his neck. She knelt beside him and cupped his chin, raising his face to make sure he was okay. His deep blue eyes locked on hers. They were filled with sadness and defeat.

"Dora, would you be so kind as to take Kieron to his room, and make sure he is okay?" Lady Lascher asked.

"Sure." Dora nodded and helped Kieron stand. She draped his arm over her shoulders, so he could rest his weight on her before she guided him out of the room.

"No! That little shit doesn't deserve a fucking nursemaid." Lord Lascher jumped in front of Dora, blocking their path to the exit. "Give him to me!" The wicked gleam in Lord Lascher's bloody eyes made her grip Kieron tighter against her. *Like hell I'm letting you near him.*

Kieron groaned, and his muscles trembled under her hands as he attempted to stand up straight on his own. "Round two," he muttered.

"Like hell!" Dora tightened her grip on Kieron. She refused to let him get hurt again. "Lord Lascher, no offense, but get the fuck out of my way before I kill you again!" she said.

Lord Lascher laughed. "Without a staff, dear? What exactly do you think *you* can do to me?"

Dora scowled at him. "Keep pissing me off and find out."

Lord Lascher poked a sharp claw into Kieron's chest, causing another bloody wound to appear on it. Kieron groaned, and Dora tried to pull him out of the demon's reach, but Lord Lascher just poked Kieron harder in the chest.

"Doodlysquat!" She screamed at Lord Lascher, but nothing happened.

The bloody claw left Kieron's chest and gently lifted her chin. "You only have the power I give you, stupid girl." Lord Lascher mocked her.

"Enough!" Lady Lascher bellowed. An invisible force flung Lord Lascher back against the wall, knocking over a china cabinet in the process. Thick green vines wrapped around his body and pinned him to the wall, so he resembled struggling wall art instead of a scary demon.

"Dora, if you'll see to Kieron, I'll see to my husband," Lady Lascher said in a calm voice. She turned towards Lord Lascher, and green smoke filled the room.

"Thanks," Dora said before rushing from the room, taking Kieron with her.

"Lionel, we need to have a chat." She heard Lady Lascher snarl as she closed the door behind her.

# 26

## SOUL SEARCHING

Dora leaned Kieron over his bed, taking great care as she helped him lay down on it. He looked beaten in every sense of the word with bruises beginning to show around his throat, deep gashes down his torso and a few cuts on his face.

He turned his face away from her and looked at the red wall of his bedroom without saying a word. She suspected he was in a lot of pain.

In an attempt to end the awkward silence, she patted him on the shoulder in a spot unmarred by injuries. It was the only part of him undamaged by the fight. "I'm going to find some bandages," she said.

"Fine." His voice sounded abrupt and serious. He didn't even glance at her, which worried her more than his wounds did.

"I'll be back in a minute." She rushed into the bathroom, searching for a first aid kit or bandages in the mahogany cabinets hanging on the wall. In the first cupboard, she found an array of man products. She eyed them with curiosity. Masculine-looking gels, aftershaves, razors and weird-looking brushes filled the cupboard. *Bloody hell, he has more of this stuff than I do.*

She shook her head. Browsing through his toiletries was not why she was here. She moved on to the second cabinet. When she opened it, her eyes widened and her mouth dropped open. Boxes and boxes of condoms in all kinds of colors and flavors were bursting out of the cupboard. *Well, at least he's well prepared ... Who uses that many condoms in a year?*

She peered back through the open doorway into his bedroom, wondering how many girls he'd slept with this year. Out of curiosity, she picked up one of the boxes. It was a black box labeled 'STUD'. It had a picture of a horse on it with the words, 'Ride all night long' emblazoned across the front. She frowned. *Eww!* She inspected the sell by date on the box and grinned. It went out of date two years ago and was unopened. *He's not a player after all.*

Dora realized she was wasting time. She quickly put the box back into the cabinet before moving on to the next one. The third cabinet had a first aid kit in it, so she grabbed it and ran back to Kieron's bedside.

Kieron turned away from her when she knelt beside his bed. She opened the first aid kit and pulled out several bandages.

"Don't bother," he muttered into his pillow as he rolled over.

"Come on, *stud.* Stop being such a baby, and let me help you," she replied without thinking. She was sure it had sounded funnier in her head. But aloud and in the silent room, it was less amusing.

He didn't move. *Fuck!*

"I'm sorry, Kieron. Sometimes my mouth opens, and I have no control over what comes out of it. I'm worried about you. Let me make sure you're okay."

"I'll be fine." His muffled voice replied. The muscles in his back tensed in stubborn refusal.

"Kieron Lascher, if you don't roll over right now, I'm going to …" She paused, trying to think of something that would tempt him to turn around. "To put my shirt back on, and you'll never see me topless."

Kieron rolled over in an instant with wide, shocked eyes until they encountered her black T-shirt. His eyes narrowed to slits. "Tease." He grumbled.

"Probably, yes. Now lay still," she said as she dabbed at the gashes in his chest with an antiseptic wipe. Most of the bleeding had stopped, leaving raw wounds. He winced every time she touched his chest, and his muscles tensed and jerked.

Dora wiped away the blood and managed to clean the wounds without making him yelp too often, but he did shriek a few times. The gashes were long red lines in his chest that weren't deep, but they leaked tears of blood again after she cleaned them. She opened several packets of sterile dressings and placed them over the clean wounds. Next, she taped them to his chest with surgical tape before pausing to examine his torso.

Once all the wounds were cleaned and covered, and the bleeding had almost stopped, she noticed his tanned chest appeared even more bronzed next to the white dressings. She found her eyes drawn to his defined muscles. *I'm just checking his breathing.* She told herself as she watched his pectorals rise and fall. She almost believed it too.

"What's wrong?" Kieron glanced down at his chest.

She coughed and looked away from his mesmerizing chest. "Um, nothing, I was just checking I didn't miss anything," she replied in her most innocent voice, pretending to be packing the bandages back into the first aid kit. *Bad Dora, stop checking out the patient's hotness.* "Right, let's look at your face." *Are we going to be drooling on that too?* A sarcastic voice in the back of her mind asked.

"My face. Why, what's wrong with it?" He widened his eyes in surprise.

"It's okay. You just have a nasty cut under your eye that I need to look at. You'll be fine." She leaned over his face, fighting off any romantic notions to stare into his eyes and forcing herself to look at the wound under them instead.

She studied the cut under his eye and forgot how sexy his body was as she leaned closer to him, frowning. There was something white poking out of the gash under his left eye. She vaguely noticed his arms had wrapped around her waist, but it didn't register with her brain. "There's something in there." She wiped at the cut, paying it careful attention.

He winced, and his hands around her waist tightened their grip. "Oww!"

"Sorry," she said, distracted by the small white object jutting out of his cheek. *I hope that isn't bone, or I'm going to barf.*

With shaking fingers, she carefully plucked the object out of his face. She sighed with relief when she realized it was just a chip of plaster, probably from the wall that Kieron and his father had crashed through. Blood flowed out of the gash, so she quickly cleaned it and pressed a sterile dressing over it. "I think you're going to live." She smiled at him, taping the dressing down.

Her eyes locked onto a pair of ocean-blue ones. Kieron gazed up at her with a wounded expression. She became aware of his hard body beneath her, and her skin tingled with anticipation. His warmth seeped through her clothes. She could feel his large hands resting on her waist, holding her against him. The combination of his vulnerable expression and tantalizing closeness, invoked feelings she had never noticed before. She shivered in his arms.

It struck her that Kieron was, and always had been, *her* demon lord. She realized he'd just been slapped around by a bigger demon. Although she didn't know why they had fought, she knew him well enough to realize it was probably for a good reason. He needed her, and the feeling made her emotions spin out of control. She wanted to kiss him and make it all better. She wanted to make him happy. She wanted to save him for once.

Dora leaned over him and brushed her lips against his. She hovered unsurely above him. *Maybe he feels like crap and doesn't want to kiss me right now?*

One of his hands cupped the back of her head and pressed her closer to him as he kissed her back. *On the other hand, maybe he does.*

His kisses were soft and light as their lips danced with each other in tentative nips. She rested her weight on her hands, so she didn't crush his chest when he pulled her closer and kissed her harder. She arched her body against his. Shivers of pleasure rippled up her spine when his warm hand roamed up and down her back.

He rolled her over on the bed, still holding her and kissing her with more urgency. Their bodies became entwined in a passionate embrace. Her heart raced, and her insides were on fire as she trailed her fingers over his bare shoulders and up the back of his neck to run them through his hair.

He jerked back and yelped when she touched his neck. *Aww shit.* She'd forgotten about his wounds. "Sorry," she mumbled and attempted to kiss him again, but he leaned away from her, frowning. She ended up pouting into the air instead.

"What's got into you?" he asked.

"What do you mean?" She tried to unscramble the confusion in her mind. *I thought he liked me?*

"You don't like kissing me." He narrowed his eyes with suspicion.

"I don't know," she replied. "Maybe I changed my mind."

His frown deepened. "Maybe you've been possessed?"

"I am not fucking possessed!" She snapped. Was this

going to be an ongoing problem in her life? Was he going to try exorcizing her next? Her fear and anger over her past clouded her thoughts. Was Kieron going to turn out to be just the same as her parents?

"Possessed people always say that." He rolled off the bed and refused to look at her.

"Are you shitting me? I …" She paused. Hell would freeze over before she told him she liked kissing him. "I felt sorry for you. That's all."

Dora climbed off the bed and headed for the door. Kieron must have stood up quickly because he grabbed her arm as she passed him and spun her around, so she fell into his chest.

"What the fu—" She didn't finish because his lips clamped down on hers. He kissed her with fiery passion, constraining her against his hard body. She struggled out of his embrace, which was more of a punishment than a kiss, and eventually broke away. "Dude, what the fuck?" She slapped him across the face before stepping away from him.

He scowled at her. "Something's not right," he said, staring at her as if she'd just grown horns.

"Yeah, I think your dad knocked you senseless!" She stormed out of the room slamming the door behind her.

"No, that's not it," she heard him say through the closed door.

*What an asshole.* Dora ran down the hall to her own room, feeling a moment of satisfaction as she slammed another door behind her. *I'm such an idiot! Why did I kiss him?*

Kieron stared at the closed door after it slammed behind Dora. He tried to call her back, but something strange was happening inside his body. It was something he'd never felt before. It brought about so many questions, and he couldn't think straight. He shook his head in an attempt to clear it as devilish sensations from having Dora in his arms tingled under his skin.

Something had happened when she kissed him, and it had set off a chemical reaction inside his body. He paused, trying to diagnose the feeling. It was as if a door had opened inside his mind, allowing him to see and feel everything. It was strange and scary, and it made no sense. As a demon, usually everything made sense. Cause and effect—want and take. There were no gray areas in evil, just pitch black. When Dora kissed him, it was as if she had changed what he was. He couldn't describe it, but he knew one thing for certain. He'd felt Dora's soul, and it was fragmented as if it was being chipped away at. He'd sensed her soul disappearing!

No demon could feel a soul; some could see them, but to feel a soul you had to be … you had to be human!

He sat down on his bed in shock. *Did she make me into a fucking human?*

He decided to test his theory and forced anger to well up inside him until it pooled in the back of his throat. It was easy to generate anger now. He just had to think about his father taking Dora away from him to make his demon form pop to the surface. He glanced in the mirror on the wall in front of him and noticed his eyes were glowing red. He touched the top of his head and felt his horns. At least they were still there. *So, I'm still a demon, but I have human powers now too?*

Kieron shook his head, and his demon form faded away. It made no sense, but *something* in him had changed when Dora kissed him. When he'd felt her heart pounding against his chest, he'd seen inside her soul. He'd seen her losing her soul!

He frowned. He didn't know who was more messed up by it all, him or Dora, but he knew he wasn't letting anymore of her soul get taken. The strange tingly feeling inside him gave him doubts. *Does this mean I have a soul now too?*

"Dude, you suck at romancing the ladies," Pooey said as he wandered into the room.

"What would you know about it?" He scowled at Pooey.

The little brown demon brushed purple fairy dust out of his hair and winked. "I never kiss and tell."

## CAVE OF SINNERS

Kieron eyed Dora from the other side of the elevator, feeling cautious of her for the first time. She was facing forward and staring at the doors. There was a frown on her face. He realized she was clearly anxious for the doors to open as he watched her clench her hands into fists. Who could blame her? The atmosphere in the elevator was icily silent.

He glanced at his father, who stood in front of them both with his back to them. Anger bubbled in his belly at the sight of his father's back. He tried to ignore the feeling, but the images of his father laughing as he strangled him refused to leave his thoughts. *This is a bad idea.*

Kieron's mother had promised him everything would be fine when she instructed him to come to the office with his father today. At first, he had refused. But when he found out Dora was going, he had eventually conceded. He refused to leave her alone with his father, regardless of how coldly she acted towards him.

He glanced at Dora again. They hadn't spoken since their kiss. It didn't look as if they would be anytime soon since she had only offered him brief, moody glances so far today. *I need to talk to her while we are alone. She doesn't understand what's happening to her.*

The elevator pinged. "Welcome to Sinners Level. Please mind your step." A metallic voice said.

Kieron stared in awe at the scene through the elevator doorway. In the distance, volcanoes shot out fiery bursts of glowing lava that flowed into a bubbling river of fire fifty-feet below them. In front of them, a narrow path bridged the elevator to the cavernous entrance of a massive black volcano. The path was a stone ledge that was only three-feet wide. On either side of it was a long drop into the glowing lava-lake below.

Lord Lascher turned around and smiled. "Watch your step, kids." He motioned for Dora to go first. She flashed him a tight smile before taking a tentative step onto the path.

Kieron took a step forward to follow her, but his father got there first, pushing him out of the way and leaving him to take up the rear. He shook his head and scowled at his father's back before following the group out on to the narrow path.

He glanced down at the lake of fire below, and beads of sweat popped up on his brow. *If I'm part human now, does it mean I can die?* For the first time in his life, he felt a moment of real fear. He didn't like the feeling.

"Today we're going to be seeing the worst of sinners.

The greedy, selfish and those who betray." Kieron's father told Dora.

She glanced back and smiled at him. "Isn't that half the planet?"

"More like, seventy-three-point-five percent of it." Lord Lascher corrected her.

"Is that going to be on the exam?" Dora's eyes widened.

"No, no. It's just an office statistic."

Kieron tuned out the conversation. *How am I going to speak to her alone, on here?* He watched her long legs stride down the path towards the cavernous entrance ahead of them, becoming hypnotized by the sight. *Damn it, Minx-witch!*

He didn't notice his father fall back until he stood beside him, which on the narrow path was a squeeze. "Kieron, we need to talk," his father whispered.

"Sure, can we do it once we're inside the cave?" he muttered, walking a little faster to overtake his father and follow Dora.

"That might not be possible." His father's voice whispered in his ear. "Just know that everything I do, no matter how cruel it may seem, is for your own good, son."

Kieron frowned. *What's he on about now?*

Something hard slammed him in the side, knocking him off the ledge. It happened so quickly, he didn't have time to scream. He went from walking on the ledge to falling towards the burning liquid below in an instant. "Dora!" he cried, but the hot blasts of wind slamming against him drowned out his words as he plummeted towards the bubbling lava.

In desperation, he clawed at the rough stone of the walkway, trying to find anything to hold onto. His skin heated up as he fell closer to the lake. *This is it, I'm going to die.*

He jerked to an abrupt halt as one of his hands gripped a jutting out ledge of rock. He clung to it with his feet dangling precariously over the fires. His heart raced, and adrenaline pumped through his veins. He peered up at his father. The demon lord was walking behind Dora on the ledge above as if he didn't have a care in the world. *Son of a bitch!*

Kieron's arms ached from holding his weight, but he ignored the feeling as anger boiled inside him. He sensed his body changing into demon form and used the extra power to pull himself up onto the small ledge with a growl. He stared up at the path, feeling his eyes burn when he saw his father put an arm around Dora as he led her into the Cave of Sinners.

The sensation of Lord Lascher's arm around her shoulders made Dora uncomfortable as he led her off the precarious path and into a dark tunnel. She glanced back and looked for Kieron, but he wasn't there. "Where's Kieron?" She frowned.

"Oh, his mother called. He had to teleport home. He'll meet up with us later," Lord Lascher replied.

"Called?" She had never seen Kieron carrying a phone.

Lord Lascher tapped her gently on the forehead with his index finger, and she noticed how long and sharp his fingernails were. "We use telepathy here."

"Ohh." She nodded. That made sense, but something didn't, and it nagged at her. "Wait, why didn't we just teleport here in the first place?"

"Well, isn't it obvious?" Lord Lascher replied.

She shook her head.

"You can't teleport, yet."

"Oh, I see." She shrugged. *I guess that's something else I need to learn.* She was annoyed with Kieron. He hadn't even said goodbye, but he had been acting funny since they'd kissed. *Maybe he was happy to have an excuse to get away from me?* She frowned again. *Asshole!*

"Come. Let me show you the deepest, darkest side of Hell." Lord Lascher stepped in front of her and motioned for her to follow him.

She glanced back at the empty path, feeling a moment of sadness because Kieron had abandoned her so easily. *Screw it! I don't need him or anyone.* She shrugged and followed Lord Lascher through the dark tunnel.

Hollow screams echoed down the tunnel, making her wince when she heard them. Firelight flickered in the distance, and the walls were made of dark volcanic rock.

At the end of the tunnel, she saw an open-plan office surrounded by a cage made of twisted steel. She drew closer to the barbed spikes of the enclosure, frowning when she noticed flames reflected in the metal. She peeked down the left side of the tunnel and saw a river of volcanic lava fuelling the fires of Hell. It burned brightly in the distance. *So this is where the sinners end up.*

She turned back to the barbed cage and peered through the holes into the room inside the prison. It looked a lot like a normal office, in some ways. There were people sitting at desks who were typing away at computer terminals. At the front of the room, a table was overflowing with a huge pile of books. Some were leather bound tomes, others flimsy paperbacks.

She noticed demons walking freely outside the cage, but the workers were trapped inside it. The workers appeared to be oblivious to the activity outside of their small confines.

While she stared at the inhabitants of the barbed cell, the lighting in the office faded from fluorescent white to murky red.

"Now the fun begins," Lord Lascher said with a gleeful glint in his dark eyes.

"What is this?" Dora asked as the workers ceased typing and turned towards the table piled up with books.

"These are the worst of people from a place nearly devoid of humanity—the dark underbelly of the internet," Lord Lascher said. "This section is for those who hurt books. It is home to pirates, anti-marketers and troll reviewers. In life, they killed author's babies. In Hell, they must repent."

"They killed babies?" Dora scowled at them. She hoped they got what they deserved.

"In a manner of speaking." Lord Lascher grinned, and his fangs glinted with an orange glow from the firelight.

She watched the office to see what happened next and jumped when the first book opened and wailed. It sounded like a baby squealing, and the sound sent tremors down her spine. Another book opened, then another. The squealing cries of babies filled the air as the workers rushed to the table, each one grabbing a book and cradling it in their arms, trying anything to stop them screaming.

The baby books were not easily satisfied. They wailed and snapped at the individual workers. Dora watched one old lady cradling her book and singing to it. The leather bound tome hushed. "Shh, little baby. Yes, that's right. Good baby book," she murmured to it, holding it close to her face.

The book gurgled at her. She smiled down at it, making soft calming noises. The book hiccupped and threw-up in her face. Milky baby-book puke splattered across her face, covering her horn-rimmed glasses. "Why you unedited piece of crap!" She screamed at it, poking it with one of her knitting needles. The book spat more puke at her before blasting out a loud scream. All the other books, which had been calming down, began wailing again too.

"God damn reviewers!" One of the other workers complained before yelping as her baby book bit her hand.

Dora watched another worker screaming as his book peed on him. He dropped the wailing book and yelped. "Sock puppet, give me a sock puppet!" The skin on his hands bubbled and peeled off, turning into painful-looking pustules. He fell to his knees crying and begging as the skin all over his body burned off.

Dora winced as he pleaded. "Please, someone help me. I'm sorry. I lied on the forums because my penis is tiny. Please give me a sock puppet." Trails of snot hung from his crooked nose in long, stringy strands as he lay on the floor wailing.

A small, furry troll scurried out from underneath one of the desks. It was about the size of a baby and wore a sock over its face with eyeholes cut in it. The troll stood over the cowering man, unfastened its tiny troll pants and peed on him.

"Thank you, yes!" He told the troll as its pee cured his bubbling skin and restored it to perfect condition. When the sock puppet had finished, it scurried away and disappeared under a desk.

"What did these people do to deserve this?" Dora asked Lord Lascher. They didn't appear to be particularly pleasant people, she noted as they tried everything from slapping the baby books to spitting on them to try and silence them.

"You have to understand what the place they come from is. It is a place devoid of empathy, compassion and humanity. It attracted the worst of humans to it. The question that may be better asked is; *what didn't they do?*" Lord Lascher pointed to a young man who was strangling his baby book. "That one killed a million author babies in his lifetime and a few authors too. He was known for making a sixteen-year-old author kill herself. He was immensely proud of that. He used to laugh and joke on the forums about *killing babies* all the time."

Dora narrowed her eyes at the man. Being bitten by

a baby book didn't feel like enough punishment for these people. "Why would anyone do that?"

"When humanity is removed, people will do anything," Lord Lascher replied. "That's why we love the internet so much. Compassion isn't something we have to worry about there. It's a place where people can be as evil as they want to be. They're doing a stellar job of selling their souls on the publishing industry. Authors attacking each other for a dime, literally a dime! Who knew souls could come so cheap? People attacking other people so they can feel important. Greed, pride and let's not forget sloth, for they can do it all from their armchairs while indulging in a takeout. It's so beautiful, I'm jealous I didn't create it myself." A tear of appreciation shone in Lord Lascher's eye.

He wiped it away and continued. "But of course, after all that sin, there is always the punishment, which is when they end up here. What punishment do you think they should have?" he asked. A devilish smile grew on his face.

Dora burned with hatred for these awful people. "I want them all to burn," she muttered.

Lord Lascher laughed with a glint of delight shining in his eyes. "And so they shall."

# 28

## FATHER'S DAY

"Kieron D. Lascher, how dare you come home in such a state?" Lady Lascher shrieked.

Kieron glanced down at the burnt rags he wore, which had once been his clothes. He raised his eyes and stared at his mother in disbelief. "Are you shitting me?"

"I did not raise you to speak to your mother like that." His mother held a hand to her mouth in shock.

"You didn't raise me, Nanny Simpson did." He grumbled.

"That demon was the worst influence on you. *I* raised you to come home looking respectable, not like some … some—"

"Someone who's been pushed into a lava lake before having to climb Mount, *Fucking* Doom to get out?" Kieron shouted.

"There's no need to shout." His mother complained.

"There is every need to shout. Where the hell is my

bloody father?" He growled.

"He's not bloody."

"He will be."

"Don't blame your father for your own mistakes."

"How is *this,* my mistake?" He gestured to his ragged jeans, which were still smoking in places.

"You follow that stupid girl around like a dog on a leash. How did you expect it to end?" His mother snapped.

"Dora? What do you mean end?" His pulse raced. "Where is she? Where's dad?"

His mother peered around his room, refusing to meet his eye. She glanced at the desk, the floor, anywhere but at him. "You really should tidy this room up," she said.

"Where is she?" he shouted.

"There's no need to keep shouting like that. Honestly, I don't know what's wrong with you lately. She's clearly been a bad influence on you."

"Answer me!"

"Fine! She's been sent home."

A shuffling noise coming from the doorway interrupted the conversation. He glanced over to see Pooey making his way out of the room, behind his mother.

"And, she left her crap behind!" Lady Lascher shouted as she spun around and pointed to Pooey, who froze in his tracks.

Pooey slowly turned around and pointed to himself, wearing an innocent expression. "Is she talking about me?"

"I suppose we'll just have to make use of him at the next barbecue."

Pooey's fluffy face scrunched up to appear even more squashed than usual. His eyes became slits as he blurted out a threatening growl. "Like fuck you will."

"What exactly are you going to do to stop me?" Kieron's mother went from calm to insane in an instant. She launched herself at Pooey, who daintily sidestepped out of her way, causing her to crash face first into Kieron's desk instead. She pushed herself up and spun around with speed and agility she should not have possessed. Her curly hair draped over her face in a mess. Her narrowed eyes glowed green, which clashed with the red stripe across her forehead from her encounter with the edge of the desk.

Pooey studied Lady Lascher for a moment before yelping and scurrying behind Kieron's legs to hide from her.

"Just for that, you're going to suffer a painful death." Lady Lascher snarled.

"Pooey is under my protection," Kieron said, his mind brimming with questions. *Dora's been sent home, back to Earth, why?*

"You're not allowed any pets." His mother snapped, ducking left and right in an attempt to close in on Pooey, who was digging his claws into the back of Kieron's shins.

"Fine, I'll just tell the Demonic Tax Authorities that dad's been holding back on his tax returns for the last five-hundred years," Kieron replied.

"You wouldn't!" His mother gasped.

"I fucking would."

"I don't know what's got into you lately, but fine! Keep your ugly mutt—"

"Hey!" Pooey grumbled. "I'm a pedigree."

"Do pieces of crap come in pedigree?" Lady Lascher taunted.

"I dunno. Look in a mirror sometime and ask yourself," Pooey replied.

Kieron groaned when green smoke billowed around his mother and her bipolar other half snarled. "Should I call the DTA now or when Dad gets home?"

Lady Lascher hissed, scowling at both Kieron and Pooey. "Fine, keep your inbred critter for now. You're grounded for a decade!" She screamed before slamming her way out of the room with green smoke curling ominously under her dress.

Kieron sank onto his bed and stared at the closed door. How could they take Dora away without telling him? What was he going to do now?

The bed bounced when Pooey jumped onto it, and he sat beside him. "What are we gunna do now?"

"What can we do?"

"You don't really believe they sent her back to Earth, do ya?"

"Why would they lie?"

"Er, because they're evil demons."

"Aren't we all? Maybe Dora's safer where she is?"

"Then why are pieces of her soul still inside Lord Fucknut's vault?"

Kieron scowled. Pooey was right. If Dora had been sent home, it would have been with her whole soul, not a fractured one.

"How do you know what's in the vault?"

"I like to explore." Pooey flashed innocent eyes at Kieron before he found a sudden interest in examining his claws.

"So, where did they send Dora?"

Pooey shrugged. "When did you last see her?"

"Going into the Cave of Sinners ..." His eyes widened. "They can't have put her in there!"

"Oh yeah, 'cause they're such compassionate souls." Pooey shook his head.

"Time moves differently there. A few hours will feel like years to Dora. They're not going to get away with it." He clenched his fists.

"What are we going to do?"

"We're going to break into the vault." He scowled at the door. This time he was going to hit his parents where it really hurt, in their bank balance.

Dora crossed her legs and uncrossed them. She eyed up the cell door, waiting for the ghoulish guard to stroll by again. He did so every hour, holding a burning torch in one hand and a bloody ax in the other. She didn't know why she waited for him, other than it was the only way to tell how many hours she'd been in the cell for.

The first hint of the guard's arrival was the clinking of chains as he dragged them across the stone floor behind him. She frowned when she saw him through the bars.

His ragged skin was ripped with old scars on it. Her stomach turned over as she studied his gray tinged flesh and the purple welts on it. Half of the skin on his jaw was missing, baring skeletal teeth on one side of his face in a gruesome grin. One of his eyes hung from the socket, and he was completely bald. He wore a ripped leather tunic with thick chains wound around him. She shivered at the chains around his fists. *Those will hurt if he hits me.*

At first, she had thought Lord Lascher was joking when he told her she wasn't coming back to Castle Lascher with him. Because Lionel had been smiling so pleasantly at her when he had left her here, it had taken her a while to realize he had meant it. He had told her that Kieron didn't want her to return with him, and since she wasn't helping improve Kieron's chances of passing the Judgment Day tests, it was for the best if she stayed here.

She had been too upset to respond. It was the kiss. It had to be. Kieron had obviously been angry with her, but she had never expected him to abandon her in Hell because of it. *I'm such an idiot!*

Lord Lascher had been kind. Well, if you could call leaving her in a prison kind. He had given her advice about her own test. He told her to use this time to become strong, and to learn to defend herself. Because, as of right now, it was the only protection she had. He hadn't lied to her. He'd told her straight. If she didn't fight back, she'd die here. Then he had left, and she had been alone with her thoughts. They weren't pleasant thoughts.

Thirteen times the guard had strolled past her cell.

For thirteen hours, she had tried to come to terms with the fact that no one was coming to save her this time. She was on her own. It was a daunting realization. *You would think I'd be used to people letting me down by now.* But she hadn't been prepared for this. She had become used to Kieron protecting her. She had forgotten how much scarier everything could be on your own, and she had forgotten how to take care of herself.

Dora stood up feeling determined and paced her cell. She refused to be defeated by a bad boy and a ropey prison cell. The tests were coming up, and she was on her own. She needed to learn to fight here and to forget about everyone else. Whatever they had in store for her, she could handle it. She scanned the room for a weapon of some kind. It was bare except for a rickety, metal bed and a bucket.

She picked up the bucket and weighed it in her hands. It had some weight in it and was durable. Okay, it wasn't a baseball bat, but it might do enough damage if she hit something with it.

She dropped the bucket when she heard a key rattling followed by a loud creak as the door opened behind her. She didn't know what to expect when she spun around, but the man standing before her was the last person she thought would walk into her cell.

She froze, speechless as her father strolled into the room and slammed the cell door shut behind him. *How is he here?* "Dad?" She couldn't believe her own eyes.

He turned towards her with red glowing eyes. *Did he die? Was he sent to hell?*

"DEMON!" He bellowed.

"Look who's talking." Dora scowled as fiery hate burned in her belly.

Chains sprang out of the walls and wrapped around her body on their own. Similar to twisting snakes, the metal bonds wound around her body and bound her to the spot. She heard crunching under her feet and peered down expecting to see stone slabs but found herself standing on a wooden pyre.

*What the fu—*

"Bitch, bitch, burn the witch." Her father sang at her. He had acquired a burning torch, from the ether it seemed, and held it in his hands as he walked towards her.

"No, no, no. This can't be happening!" she cried. But it was happening, she realized as he lit the wood beneath her feet. He was going to burn her, and this time there was no one to save her.

Heat scorched her skin as the flames grew. Her father became a dark shadow on the other side of the fire. She could feel her skin bubbling as the blaze grew. She screamed in agony. *I'm dead. This time I'm dead!* The flames licked at her skin, but all she could do was shriek in pain and terror. She could hear her father laughing in the background. "Kieron," she whimpered. "Where are you?" Her heart ached, and something dark entered her soul as the world around her faded to black.

When Dora awoke, she was alone and unharmed in her cell. The ghoulish guard walked by again, dragging his chains behind him. She sat up and checked her arms. Her skin was unblemished, but she was trembling in fear. *Did*

*I burn? Am I dead now?*

She jerked her head around when she heard keys jangling in the cell door. Her father walked into the room and slammed the door shut behind him.

"Incinerato!" she shouted, pointing her hands at him. A fireball shot from her fingers and hit him squarely in the chest. He stumbled backwards against the door as he ignited into a ball of flames. He stepped forward and continued towards her as if he could not feel the flames engulfing him. His eyes glowed red at her. "DEMON!" He bellowed.

*Aww fuck. Not again.*

## 29

## THE PIT POCKET HEIST

Kieron watched in silence through the keyhole of the door as his mother strode across his father's office. He was hidden inside his father's stuffy stationary cupboard next to the main office.

"Let me see," Pooey whispered in his ear as the little demon climbed up his arm and sat on his shoulder, trying to push his head away from the keyhole with his fluffy, little paws.

Kieron violently shook his head, attempting to silence and dislodge the fluffy fiend at the same time. When Pooey refused to budge, he lifted his arm and pushed Pooey off his shoulder. *Not now, something is finally about to happen.* His eyes remained glued to the scene in the adjoining room.

"You shouldn't have taken her soul." He heard his mother's voice echo through the door as he watched her pace the room through the keyhole. She stopped and stared at his father with venom in her eyes.

"But it was so shiny," Lord Lascher replied. He reclined back in his chair and rested his feet on the desk. "What does it matter anyway? She'll be back on Earth in no time."

"It matters, you idiot, because she might do well in the tests without a soul. The whole purpose of summoning her here was to help Kieron pass his Judgment Day exams. And it would have worked too if you hadn't been greedy." Lady Lascher shot a bolt of electricity at her husband and slapped him in the face with it. He slammed back in his chair, which flipped over dropping him on to the floor with a loud thud.

"Idiot!" Lady Lascher repeated.

Kieron watched his father stand up, rubbing his head. Little blue sparks of electricity shot off his hair, repeatedly zapping him and making him jump.

*Is this true? They brought Dora here, so she would be an easy competitor for me to beat in the final battle. She was brought here, so I could cheat my exams...*

He frowned. When it came to his parents, he didn't have very high expectations, but he was disappointed they had managed to fool him so easily. He hadn't been even mildly suspicious, but he should have been. A portal had magically opened, and he'd never suspected why it was there. His magic hadn't worked the way it should have on Earth, and he'd known it had felt restricted. He groaned when he realized why his spells had not all worked on Earth. He'd had a parental restriction on his powers when he was there. *Son of a bitch! I was set up.*

Dora shouldn't have any powers in Hell—she was

just a human. When you summon water, it rarely turns into bird shit. It wasn't his magic that had done any of it. His mother had guided them here!

"I only took a bit of her soul." Lord Lascher whined.

"You took more than half of it! I spoke to Kahn, and he said she is looking like a good competitor. She has already flayed two demons. I imbued her with my power, but she was never supposed to learn to use it! With a soul intact she wouldn't have, but now ..." Lady Lascher shook her head. "She could be as powerful as me!"

"Take the power back." Lord Lascher shrugged.

"You know I can't do that. The judges will notice her weakness."

"Well, I can't put her soul back! Only ..." Lord Lascher paled and appeared queasy. "Angels can do that, and I'm not dealing with those self-righteous fuckers again."

"If Kieron loses to her, I'm going to exile *you* to Earth." Lady Lascher shot her husband a dark look before storming out of his office.

"Don't be like that, sweetheart." Kieron watched his father jump out of his chair and chase after his mother. "We can work this out." He heard his father call out as he left the office.

Kieron rolled around and sat on the floor, resting his back against the door in defeat. Dora was only here so she could lose to him on Judgment Day. *Half of her soul has been siphoned away! That is why she has been acting so weird lately—my father has been taking her soul.*

"So ..." Pooey stood in front of him with his hands

227

on his hips. "What are we gunna do now?"

"I don't know." He shook his head. Even if he got her soul back, he couldn't put it back in her. And even if he could, one way or another he'd lose her. She was either going to be exiled to Earth, or he was.

*It's better that she's herself, wherever she is. I don't care what happens to me.* He nodded. However it turned out, the most important thing was restoring her soul. Dora would be okay anywhere as long as she was herself.

Pooey narrowed his eyes. "What are you smiling about?"

"I've just figured out what we're going to do."

"Does it involve you saving your own ass?" Pooey's eyes became slits.

"What? No! We are going to put back Dora's soul. I mean, wherever she ends up, she needs that right? So, the first thing we're going to do is get her soul and put it back in her."

"And what happens on Judgment Day?"

"I dunno. I'll think of something."

"Famous last words," Pooey muttered.

"No matter what happens, she's better off with her soul, right?"

"Yeah, I guess. Know a lot of angels do ya? I sure as hell don't."

"Um, well I met one once. It was before he became an angel, and he's a bit … different," Kieron mumbled.

"Different how?"

"Well, he was in limbo for a while. They weren't certain where he should go. He ended up in Heaven and went up the ranks there, but I guess everyone has a past."

"I thought they washed your sins away?" Pooey scratched his head and appeared confused.

"Yeah, but … well, let's just say he needed a thorough scrubbing."

"Where is he?"

"That's the hard part. I think he's in Heaven. Finding him won't be easy."

"How'd you meet him?"

"He knew my mother when I was just a demon spawn. He seemed nice though. I think he'd help us."

"Yeah, if we can find him," Pooey said. "Okay, we just need to break into an unbreakable vault for Dora's soul, and then we need to break into Heaven to find someone to put it back in her. After that, we need to get them near her on Judgment Day, which is tomorrow morning. Then, we have to work out a way to put the soul back in her without *her* killing you since she's probably now as evil as your mother is. Oh, and let's not forget that we need to stop you both being exiled by the judges, which is a near impossibility as they only answer to Satan himself." Pooey took a deep breath before continuing. "Easy pie. Good job you have a ninja on your side."

"We can do this." Kieron stood up, feeling determined as he opened the cupboard door.

"Yep, ridiculous bravado, that'll help in the face of impossibility," Pooey muttered behind him.

Kieron ignored him and stepped into his father's office. He turned towards the door of the vault and eyed the green aura billowing around it. "Any ideas?" he asked Pooey.

Pooey shrugged and appeared defeated.

"Come on! You got in there before."

"Yeah, but I'm not some hoofing great pillock am I. You're way too big to fit through the smoke rings."

Kieron eyed the green swirling smoke. He knew from experience that touching it would set off wailing alarms, and it hurt like hell. "What about if we make me smaller?"

"You'd need to be pocket-sized. And when I say pocket, I mean mine," Pooey replied. "You can't move like I can, so I'll have to carry you through."

Kieron eyed Pooey. "You don't have any pockets."

"Sure I do." Pooey lifted his fluffy arm to reveal a pocket in his armpit.

"Oh, eww! No way." Kieron shook his head in disgust.

"You know it's the only way," Pooey said.

"Of all the unholy things in this dimension ..." Kieron grumbled as he prepared to cast a shrinking spell. "This is the most disgusting one I've ever had to do." He sighed and cast the spell. "Shortass," he chanted. The world grew in size around him as he shrank to the size of a thumbnail. He peered up at Pooey, who now looked like a massive, majestic beast from this angle.

"You're so cute!" Pooey squealed at him.

Kieron put his hands on his hips and scowled.

"Stop it! The cuteness is killing me." Pooey continued.

"Will you just put me in the damn vault already?" Kieron shouted, but it came out as a squeak.

Pooey scooped him up into his massive paws and patted him on the head. "Who's a cute, little fella then? Who's my little cutie? You are, yes you are ..." Pooey rubbed him under the chin and made baby noises at him.

"Put me in your fucking pocket, *now!*" He snapped.

"Aww okay, but you're still adorable." Pooey stroked his hair before lifting him towards the pocket under his armpit.

"Yeah, well you stink." He wished he'd turned off his sense of smell with magic too. "Oh, Hell no! I'm not going in there. It reeks." He clawed at Pooey's giant hand, trying to escape the stench as he neared the armpit pocket.

"Don't be such a wuss," Pooey said.

"Agh! The smell is killing me. Get it away from me," he cried as the sweaty pocket in Pooey's armpit came closer, and the stench almost knocked him out. The pocket was brimming with fluffy fur and dripping with giant drops of sweat.

"Okay, for Satan's sake," Pooey muttered. In one swift movement, he lowered his arm and dropped Kieron into a furry fanny pack just under his belly button. "Try this one instead."

Kieron peered around the new pocket. He hadn't seen much going in, but at least it didn't smell as foul as Pooey's armpit. It was still pretty rank though.

"It smells like ass in here!" He called out, glancing around. He was standing in a cavern of fur.

"It could be worse. Hold on tight. It's gonna be a

bumpy ride," Pooey said.

"Wha—" He didn't finish his sentence as he was thrown around inside the pocket, and his head smashed against furry walls when he violently bounced off them.

"Ohh, I'm gonna barf." He gripped onto the long tendrils of fur with both his hands and braced himself against the inside of the pocket. His stomach turned over several times as he repeatedly spun around and flipped over. *What the hell is Pooey doing, backflips?*

Finally, the spinning stopped. He pulled himself upright on shaky legs, clinging to the fur to keep his balance. The pocket opened, and he inhaled a welcome breath of fresh air as Pooey scooped him out of it and placed him on the floor inside the vault.

Kieron glanced behind him at the closed vault door. It was thick iron with intricate engravings covering every inch of it. "I know how you got through the smoke alarms, but how did you get through a closed door?"

"Mouse hole." Pooey pointed to the small hole next to the locked door.

"I didn't know we had mice."

"You don't anymore." Pooey grinned and flashed his teeth.

"Eww," Kieron managed before casting the spell to grow in size. "Egotisilly!" He closed his eyes as his body returned to normal size and tried to ignore the rank smell hovering around his nostrils. "The inside of your fanny pack reeks!"

"You got off easy," Pooey grumbled.

"How so?"

"You totally ripped out half my pubes in there, man. Never again!"

Kieron's stomach flipped over on impulse. "That was your—oh, I'm gonna be sick."

Pooey shrugged. "Don't say I didn't offer you the pit-pocket." He walked deeper into the vault, picking up random boxes and looking inside them. "What's her soul look like, anyway?"

"How are we getting out of here?" Kieron ignored his question.

"Same way we got in," Pooey replied.

"Not a chance."

"Pit-pocket?"

He groaned and brushed the Pooey pubes off his clothes, which had grown in size with him and were massive tangles of crinkly fur.

"Fine, whatever, I'll remove my sense of smell before I go in it." He sighed.

"So where will Dora's soul be?" Pooey asked.

Kieron scanned the vault. It was a massive room held up by ornate pillars. Mountains of gems, gold and stacks of soul-chips lined both sides of the vault. A golden walkway stretched down the center of the room. "It could be anywhere," he said, glancing down the long room to the light at the end of it.

He saw a glowing white light at the end of the room. Something shone brightly on a pedestal in the distance. He squinted to try to see what it was, but it was just a hazy white glow to him.

"What?" Pooey asked. He turned to look in the same

direction as Kieron.

"That light," Kieron said.

"What light?"

"That one." He pointed in the direction of the white glow.

"I can't see anything."

"The glowing thing at the end of the room, you can't see it?"

"Nah mate, I think I must have flipped you over too many times."

Kieron frowned and walked towards the illumination. It was definitely glowing.

"Hey wait." Pooey ran after him. "Be wary of—"

Kieron stepped onto a metal plate embedded in the floor. It sank under his foot and made a loud clicking sound.

"Shit," Pooey muttered.

"What?"

"Booby traps."

"Oh, crap." He spun around as the sound of cogs grinding filled the room in all directions. He peered up to see the roof opening above him. He gulped when a massive black scaly claw with vicious talons broke through the thin gap in the ceiling.

Pooey stared up at it. "I do not want to find out what *that* is. Let's get outta here."

Kieron peered at the glowing light. It was as if it were calling to him. He could feel it. "Wait here." He told Pooey as he raced down the room towards the light.

"What, under the big black scary thing?" He heard

Pooey say incredulously as he left him behind.

He didn't know why, but he knew he needed the glowing object. He felt connected to it, as if it was his to protect. He couldn't explain it. He just felt it with every essence of his being.

When he reached the pedestal, he took a quick glance over his shoulder to ensure Pooey was okay. A scaly black arm reached into the room as the ceiling continued to open. Loud growls came from above, emanating from whatever was encased on top of the vault.

Kieron peered down at the glowing object. It was a pile of soul-chips, but they shone with blinding white light. He touched one and felt an overwhelming connection to them. *These must be part of Dora.*

Wasting no time, he scooped them all into a nearby gem bag and quickly tied it to his belt. He spun around to see two massive arms hanging through the growing opening in the ceiling. The arms were trying to catch Pooey, who darted around the room with incredible speed to avoid capture.

"Are you okay?" he shouted.

"Hurry the fuck up!" Pooey cried.

He raced down the room towards Pooey and the exit. He grabbed a sword out of a pile of weapons as he ran past it and charged at the left arm of the beast, aiming to cut his way through it. One of its claws snagged Pooey and pinned his little body down on the golden floor. Kieron raised his sword and roared as he raced towards it.

"Demon form!" Pooey reminded him

Kieron growled and shifted while running. Anger

and fire rushed through his veins. His horns rose, and his muscle mass grew. He launched himself at the arm holding Pooey down and slashed it with the blade. A wounded yelp echoed from above as the massive arm swiftly retracted back up into the ceiling.

Kieron stared up at the ceiling in surprise. *That was far too easy.* The massive beast had retreated. He jumped when a loud sobbing from above shattered the silence.

"What a fucking wuss," Pooey said.

Kieron turned around to smile at his small companion. He almost fell on his ass when his eyes met a big brown fluffy face attached to a six-foot tall teddy bear with wicked claws and great abs.

Kieron raised his sword on instinct. "What the hell?"

"What? It's just me," the beast said.

"Who?" He waved the sword at it to keep it at a distance.

"I'm Pooey, you idiot! This is my demon form."

"You turn into a six-foot fluffy beast on steroids?" He narrowed his eyes at the Pooey beast. Its fangs were massive. "Wait, why were you a cuddly toy at the fair? How could *you* be enslaved?"

"I have self-esteem issues." Pooey lowered his big shaggy head as he shrank.

Kieron winced. "Umm, sorry. I didn't mean t—"

"Shuddup and get in my armpit." Pooey scowled up at him.

Kieron sighed and prepared to cast a shrinking spell as the sounds of a massive scaly beast could be heard wailing above them.

He glanced at the gem bag tied to his belt. The bag glowed brightly, but Pooey appeared unable to see it. "Fine, but get this over with quickly, or I'll set your armpit hair on fire." He grumbled.

# THE NEW ME

D ora frowned at the small golden demon. "You
want me to do what?"

"Put this on, sweetie. You can't compete in
that grunge look of yours." He eyed her ripped pantyhose
and torn black dress with distaste. He dramatically flicked
blond bangs off his shiny brow. "This is the run up to
Judgment Day. All competitors win by votes, honey. If
you wanna be in the finals with the high lords, you need
to make an impact," he said, holding up a skintight pink
onesie and shaking it at her. "You wanna win, don't
you?"

"Not that badly." She scowled at him.

"Everyone's going to be dressed in red or black. You
need to stand out, make an impression. I'm thinking
pretty in pink meets white fluff. You'll be sweet, sugary
and memorable." The golden demon picked a white fluffy
scarf off the rack behind him and held it up against the
pink onesie. "If only you were blonde," he muttered.

Dora narrowed her eyes. "I know what'll work." She told him in a calm tone.

"Yes?" He glanced up with hope shining in his eyes.

She shot a fireball at him and burnt the outfit in his hands until it was a blackened rag. "Perfect," she muttered.

"No! What did you do?"

She pointed a threatening finger at the designer demon. "Get the fuck away from me, man before I burn your ass."

The demon squealed and ran out of the room. "Fine, lose and be forgotten. See if I care," he cried as he flounced out of the dressing room.

She picked up the charred remains of the onesie. It was black now with a pattern of faint pink veins that looked like marble. There were holes all over it in random places. She eyed the dressing room for accessories and smiled as she had an idea. *I'll give them something to remember.*

Dora stepped out on to the stage wearing a charcoal and marble-patterned lycra onesie. It had gaping holes burnt all over it, showing a tantalizing amount of bare skin. She grinned down at her reflection in the glass stage. The formfitting costume left little to the imagination. She'd twisted her hair up into intricate knots with gold and silver flecks of thread wound through it and decorated her face and bare skin with gold and silver war paint to match it.

She took her place on the contestant's platform and

stood tall while she waited to be called. All around her, the other contestants shifted uncomfortably in their own lackluster costumes. Especially the one in the yellow feathered bikini and stilettos—The poor guy probably wasn't used to wearing heels.

After what seemed like years, she was finally free of her cell. She didn't know how long she'd been in there for, but it had felt like forever. Time had no meaning to her anymore. When they had taken her out of her prison and brought her here, she had been informed she was ready to be judged.

She could barely remember who she had been before the Cave of Sinners. It was all vague thoughts that could be memories or could just have been thoughts. All she knew for certain was that she had to use any opportunity to escape. There was no way she was going back to her cell, and anyone who got in her way was going to die.

The competition had begun. She had already faced two demons and beaten them. She shot a sideways glance at the other competitors. To reach the finals with the high-level demons, she had to kill another contestant today. Her eyes flicked from one contestant to the next. Some were waifish things who were insane for even trying to get into Hell. Others were mean-looking demons with sharp claws and cold fury in their eyes.

Dora knew today would not be easy. It was the luck of the draw on who she would fight, but she had been training for this—she was ready. Her hands clenched into fists. Nothing was going to get in her way.

"Welcome to the semifinals of the Judgment Day

Games! Let's hear some applause for our first contestant! Yes, my hellish minions, it's the feisty fighter you all love—Deeeeemonic Dora!"

The crowds roared as she stepped off the podium and into the center of the stage. The bright spotlight shone over her and followed her movements. Her eyes flicked up to see herself on the big screen while she faced the floor. In a practiced moment of dramatics, she looked up when the music stopped and activated her spell at the same time.

Massive black wings whooshed out of her back and flapped loudly behind her on the stage, almost covering it. Sharp horns shot out of the top of her head as she faced the crowds with a grim smile. Demons and people were waving and jumping in the crowds below, going crazy for her new look. They were calling out her name and cheering for her. She flapped her huge wings, shooting a sideways glance towards the other competitors. They were wide-eyed and struggling to keep their stupid costumes in place. Gusts of wind from her wings blasted at them, sending tiaras and Las Vegas-style headdresses off their heads and into the crowds below.

Dora turned to face her audience as fireworks shot into the blood-red sky behind her. *Now they'll remember me.*

A million voices called out her name, chanting for her. "Demonic Dora, Demonic Dora ..." But one voice was out of sync.

She frowned and concentrated on trying to hear it through the screaming audience.

"Dora-minx!" A singular voice cried.

She narrowed her eyes as she studied the mass of people in the audience. She knew that name, but she couldn't remember how she knew it. Was it a memory or a dream? She searched the crowds for a face to match the voice until she noticed a blond-haired guy jumping up and down.

She focused on him and studied him from the stage. He was young and attractive. On his shoulder sat a shitty brown thing, which might have been a dog.

"Dora-minx, are you okay?" he shouted.

*Who the hell is this guy?*

She vaguely remembered the blond guy, but a fog clouded her mind. The time in her cell had not been kind to her memories. She couldn't remember if he was someone she had once known or not. He acted as if he knew her, but that didn't mean anything. It didn't matter, anyway. She had no time for friends. She shook her head and focused back on the games. He was probably just some fan boy who had her poster on his wall—he looked the type.

The audience hushed as the host of the show stepped forward wearing a sparkling white suit. He grinned at the anxious demons, making them wait for a frustratingly long time before he pulled her competitor's name out of the hat.

"Demonic Dora will be facing …" The host trailed off, keeping the demons in suspense. Some cried out, others threw fireballs at him, which he expertly dodged. After a few more minutes, he flashed his teeth. "Killer

Kahn!" he eventually cried.

She turned to face her rival. Kahn was an oafish-looking demon with sneaky eyes. He towered over her in height and in bulk. His costume was pink and fluffy, but his eyes behind the mask were sharp and black. He stepped onto the stage with a smirk on his face as Dora moved aside for his showcase introduction.

When the spotlight fell on him, he looked up while casting a scorpion tail behind him in an attempt to rip off Dora's entrance idea, but he fucked it up and ended up with a white fluffy bunny tail instead.

The crowds roared with laughter and chanted for 'Demonic Dora'. She smiled to the audience and flapped her wings. *Let the battle begin!*

"Dude, I don't think she recognized you," Pooey said. "Shouldn't we be trying to get to Heaven?"

"They're putting her through the qualifiers," Kieron replied. "You know what that means. She will not be starting as a high-level demon. She might die in the qualifiers before the exams! Screw Heaven. It won't do her any good if she's obliterated here."

"How come it changed? She was listed in the high-level demon finals last week, and now she's just a qualifying demon. What gives?" Pooey scratched his head.

"It's my fucking parents. I'll bet they exposed her and removed her status. My mother thinks she's a threat, so she's trying to have Dora removed from the top tier of the competition by killing her before she gets there." Kieron shook his head as he pushed through the crowds of demons and headed towards the qualifying arena.

"On the bright side, the guy she's fighting has the magical skills of a cabbage," Pooey added.

"Two demons enter, but only one will leave!" A voice boomed over the speakers.

Kieron looked up and groaned. "No! The fight's beginning. We need to get in there and save her." He shoved past people to get to the arena Dora was fighting in.

"She's fighting a useless lump. Don't worry," Pooey said.

"That guy's a sneaky bastard. He crippled me for four months last year," Kieron replied, glancing up at the open doors of the arena in the distance. There was no way he was going to make it. There were too many demons in the way.

"How'd he manage that?" Pooey asked.

"He er, sat on me."

"And the winner is ..." A voice blared over the speakers.

*Please be Dora, please be Dora ...*

"Deeeeeeeeeeemonic Dora!"

The crowds roared, and Kieron raced through them, knocking them over to get to the stage exit.

He gasped when he saw her coming out of the arena, held up by two guards. He growled at the state of her. She hung limply in the guards arms, and there were shallow cuts all over her body. Her hair was a ragged mess, but he was relieved to see she wasn't mortally wounded.

He raced to the edge of the barrier, aching to grab her in his arms and haul her away from this place. He was almost close enough to touch her. "Dora, are you okay?" he cried.

She glanced up at him. "You again," she murmured. She looked exhausted, and every essence of him wanted to save her right now and take her home.

He leapt at the barrier to try to get to her, but three burly guards held him back. "Let me through," he shouted. "I'm a high-level demon. Let me pass, right now!"

"Sorry sport, your game time with her is in the morning," a guard said.

"No, I mean—"

"What?" Dora scowled at him and propped herself up one of the guards. She looked Kieron straight in the eye. "So you're who I'm fighting tomorrow." Her eyes turned cold as a deadly scowl crossed her face.

He froze in terror for a moment. "No, I—am I? That's not what—"

Red smoke billowed around her, and her eyes glittered with insanity. "Don't be so eager to die. The sun will rise soon enough."

A shiver of fear shot up his spine as the guards dragged her away.

"I didn't mean that," he shouted after her.

"I did." She called behind her as the guards led her into a private room, and the door slammed shut behind them.

"Dude, you're a dead man," Pooey said.

"Shut up." Kieron snapped, even though Pooey was right. Dora wasn't herself. She was ... well, she was just like his mother. "Shit!"

"Let's just stick to the plan," Pooey said.

"We can't."

"Why not."

"I already tried to get into Heaven." Kieron admitted. "They slammed the door in my face. I don't know what to do."

Pooey frowned. "You better think of something. We only have a few hours."

"I will." Kieron stared at the closed door of the room they had taken Dora into. "There has to be a way."

# DYING ALIVE

Kieron stepped out onto the golden sands of the arena. The noise was deafening as the crowds roared. His eyes scanned across the faces of the demons in the stands. He saw a multitude of twisted expressions, and they were all baying for blood.

He searched for his parent's faces amid the masses and scowled when he found them in the front row, beneath the judge's podium. Both wore proud expressions while sitting in golden box seats cheering for him.

"Go get her, son!" his father shouted.

He ground his teeth and narrowed his eyes. He would never forgive them for this.

The crowds roared as the gate at the other end of the arena opened. Dora stepped out onto the sands.

Kieron gasped when he saw her. Tendrils of her dark hair had escaped the tribal beads around her braids and were blowing behind her in dark wisps. She had green and gold stripes painted across her face, and bloodstained leather armor clung to her curves.

Hot winds gusted across the arena, creating beads of sweat on his skin. He watched her walk towards him with panther like grace. The fierce glint in her eyes, and her battle stance made her appear like an amazon warrior—beautiful and deadly.

He tried to call out to her. "Dora, I—"

"Contenders prepare!" A hollow voice echoed around the arena.

He glanced up at the judge's balcony. There were three dark-robed figures seated on twisted golden thrones, each hidden under the shadow of their hoods with only their clawed hands visible. He wasn't even sure which one had spoken. No one knew who the judges were. They were a mystery to all who inhabited Hell.

Kieron tried to calm his taut nerves by exhaling. He shifted his eyes back at Dora. *There has to be a way to reach her.* Even though he refused to fight her, his natural instincts kicked in when he watched her tighten her grip on her staff. Her muscles tensed in preparation, and her eyes never left him. It was as if she didn't see the baying crowds, just her target—him.

He drummed his fingers on his staff. *I'm not fighting her. I don't care what they do.* That was his plan—refusing to fight. If he didn't fight, she couldn't get hurt, right?

"Let the battle commence!" The hollow voice echoed.

The crowds in the stands roared in approval. Dora sprinted across the arena with her staff raised in attack stance.

Kieron stood resolute, refusing to attack.

"At least defend yourself, you daft pillock!" Pooey's voice came from the stands behind him.

Dora slammed her staff into the sands. "Earthshatter!" she cried.

He watched in horror as the ground beneath her staff cracked in his direction, creating gaping chasms that dropped into burning lava. The cracks raced towards him, and the earth trembled and shook under his feet. He leapt across the gaps, trying to find solid ground as it fell away into the ether.

He balanced precariously on a jagged chunk of earth and held up his staff. "Sandfill!" he shouted.

The sand filled the chasms with each grain multiplying from another until the gaping cracks disappeared, and the arena floor was solid again.

"Dora, we need to talk about this," he shouted at her.

She held up her hand. For a brief moment, he thought she'd heard him, but he quickly changed his mind when spikes of ice shot from her fingers, aimed directly at him. There were thousands of icy shards, each one glinting with sharp, deadly-looking tips.

Kieron ducked and rolled, avoiding most of the blast, but several shards cut through his clothes and sliced across his skin. *I've gotta stop her, somehow.*

He curled up in agony as a stray spike of ice sliced across his waist before embedding in the wall of the stand behind him. His blood flowed through his shirt, dripping onto the sands of the arena.

He pulled off his shirt and stared down at the gash in his side. It was a deep cut. He wadded his shirt against it to slow the bleeding. By the time he glanced up towards Dora, she was already casting again with her staff. He realized he didn't have time to heal. He needed to use all his power to protect himself. "Cryosphere!" he cried.

A bubble of impenetrable glass surrounded him, protecting him from the blasts of fire she shot at him. The fire bounced around the sphere, but he was safe inside it.

The crowds booed. Defensive spells were never the popular choice.

Dora's dark eyes had become slits as she studied his protective coating. He pushed himself off the ground, using all his strength to keep up the shields against her constant attacks.

"Steroidstrong!" Dora cast upon herself before she launched herself onto his sphere with a roar. She landed on top of it on her hands and knees and peered down at him through the glass. *What the fuck is she doing?*

She drove her fist into the glass with inhuman strength again, and again. He felt every punch slam into his head as she slammed her fist into the glass barrier. The barrier had come from his mind, so it was where her punches landed. He used every essence of his power to keep her out, but the shield cracked under the pressure.

She stared down at him with pure evil in her eyes as her fist smashed through the shield. Shards of glass sprayed him as the barrier fell apart around him. She dropped onto him, pinning him to the ground with a snarl.

One glance into her cold eyes made him realize he

had lost. He knew he was mortally wounded with jagged glass impaling his legs and chest. He was drained of all of his demon power, but still fought through the pain even though he knew he couldn't win.

"Nooo!" Pooey cried from the stands.

"Kill, kill, kill!" The crowds roared.

"Now you die." Dora snarled at him.

The world blurred into a golden haze for a moment. Kieron widened his eyes with surprise when he noticed a new power appear inside him. It was something he'd never realized was there before. Now his demon powers were drained, something else had been set free. He could feel a strong and warm glow inside him—a new power.

He closed his eyes for a moment to feel this new source of energy. It was as if a dormant part of him had awoken, and it was powerful. With a roar of agony, he rolled over, taking Dora with him and pinning her to the bloody sands of the arena. His flesh tore as the sharp glass crushed into his skin, but it didn't matter. Nothing mattered but this growing power inside of him.

Dora struggled beneath him. He knew he shouldn't be able to pin her down so easily, but he could. He ripped the gem bag out of his pocket and scooped her soul-chips into his palm.

"I hate you!" she cried.

"I love you!" he shouted back before punching the soul-chips into her chest, crushing them into her heart.

Blinding white light flashed around them, and both their bodies glowed. The arena faded into the background. All Kieron could see was Dora.

251

Her skin glowed serene gold, but her eyes sparkled with dark fury. He forced himself to fight the pain and keep hold of her. His body ached with every movement, and exhaustion clouded his mind. There was a searing pain between his shoulder blades. His back throbbed as if someone had ripped out his spine. He fought for consciousness as a feeling of something powerful shot through him and ripped him apart inside. A thought crossed his hazy mind, and he realized he'd been a conduit for something not of this dimension—a conductor for something ... something good.

He leaned over Dora and kissed her. He didn't know what any of it meant, and he didn't know if he would survive, but her soft lips were the last thing he wanted to feel before he lost consciousness—and they were.

*What are you doing? Kill him! You're supposed to.* Dora stopped kissing the high-level demon and pushed him off her, onto his back. She knelt over him and pulled her knife from the scabbard at her hip, aiming it into Kieron's chest. She froze in position. *Kieron? I know him. How do I know him?*

The memory in her mind was a whisper. She frowned and tried to clear her thoughts. They had been so clear, so straightforward earlier.

Around her, she heard the crowds calling out for a kill. Her competitor lay beneath her unconscious. All she had to do was stab him, and she would win. But something wasn't right. There was a nagging feeling that something was terribly wrong. It wasn't in her nature to do what she was told. She growled at the crowds as they roared.

"Kill, kill, kill..."

*I don't want to make those assholes happy.* She pondered her options before snarling and throwing the knife away. She didn't do what other people told her to do. She never had. Not when her parents had told her to be good, and not when the demons had told her to be bad. She was free. She never did what she was told to do.

She battled against a feeling that she was throwing away her chance of winning as her memories came back to her in a flood. *Wait a minute. What the fuck am I doing?*

The memories of the guy lying beneath her filled her mind. She gasped. "Kieron!" she cried at his inert form. She grabbed his shoulders and shook him. "Kieron, wake up. Please wake up." She shook his shoulders and stared down at his face. There were nasty gashes across it, and his eyes remained closed.

She reached across the sands and grabbed her staff with her hand. "Heal!" She pointed it at Kieron, but nothing happened. She remembered everything. She knew she had done this. She had become evil, and he'd died saving her.

"HEAL!" Dora squeezed her eyes shut in concentration as she tightly gripped the staff, but nothing happened. She opened her eyes and looked around the arena in desperation. *Someone help me.* The crowds were standing in silent awe, staring down at her and Kieron. She glanced back at him and her jaw dropped open in surprise.

His skin glowed with a bright light. His hair appeared tinted with strands of gold. Massive white-feathered wings stretched out on the sands beneath him. *Kieron's a fucking angel!*

"I knew there was something weird about him." She heard Pooey shout.

"YOU SLUT!" Lord Lascher screamed from the other end of the arena. Dora glanced back, just in time to see Lady Lascher punch Lord Lasher in the face and knock him out.

Dora shook her head and stared down at Kieron. The feathers on his wings weren't all white, some were black. He was deathly still, and his eyes remained closed.

She didn't do crying. She didn't! But he'd saved her, and why couldn't she save him? She held the staff over him and waved it to try to make it work. "Heal, Kieron. Please heal," she whispered as hot tears rolled down her cheeks. "I'm sorry! Please come back."

She knew he was the only person she wanted to spend eternity with. He was the only person who didn't try to change her. He liked her for who she was. Her tears splashed onto the cuts on his face. They sizzled and disappeared, leaving unmarred skin behind.

"Come back to me." She breathed.

Kieron didn't move. She ached inside. *Don't die! Don't ...*

She knew it was too late. Whatever magic had

created Kieron did not exist here to save him. Hell only contained evil, and there was nothing evil inside him to heal. Hell magic would do nothing for him.

Dora's face creased up as the agony of losing him wracked her body. He was the only being who had ever cared about her, and he was gone.

A small paw touched her arm and she looked down to see Pooey standing beside her. "He can't be gone." She told Pooey.

"He's far too optimistic to die." Pooey sounded throaty. His big brown eyes filled with sorrow as he glanced down at Kieron.

"How can an angel die?" Dora shook her head. No, she would not give up. She grabbed Kieron's shoulders and shook him with inhuman strength. "Wake up!"

Pooey touched her arm again. "I don't think that will work."

"Tell me what will work." She begged. She needed to fix this.

"I don't fucking know. How do humans do it?"

She rubbed her eyes and stared at Kieron. His body had healed, but it appeared to be an empty shell. Her tears had restored him to perfect health, but his heart wasn't beating, and he wasn't breathing.

She stroked his face, leaned over him and kissed him. When she pulled away, she expected his eyes to open, but they didn't.

She took a deep breath and began CPR. She didn't know what she was doing, but she'd seen enough movies to give it a try. She pressed down on his muscled chest, trying to massage his heart. She leaned over and breathed air into his lungs. She returned to his chest, about to press down again, but shook her head. He wasn't breathing, and he wasn't moving. CPR wasn't going to work. She tried to think clearly, but her mind was a mess.

She caressed his cheek and hung her head. She knew she was too late. "I love you too," she whispered into his ear as she leaned over him. It was lame goodbye because he couldn't hear her. She turned to stand up and face the crowds with anger burning in her belly. Someone was going to pay for this. Hell, everyone was going to pay for it.

A strong hand grabbed her wrist. She glanced down to see Kieron's hand on her arm. Her heart leapt into her throat as she spun around to look at him. His ocean-blue eyes were open, and he was smiling at her. He wore the same wicked smile he had worn the first day they had met. "I knew you'd love me one day," he said with a wink.

Dora battled with the decision on whether to punch him or kiss him. She chose the third option, in the end and hugged him tightly against her. "Don't you ever die on me again, or I'll ... I'll kill you!"

Kieron laughed. "Don't be silly, Dora-minx. You can't kill demons."

"You're not a demon, mate," Pooey muttered.

"There's no need to insult me. Just because I've only got small horns—"

"Um." Dora interrupted and pointed to Kieron's wings.

Kieron glanced sideways briefly before looking back

at her with a confident smile. His expression froze on his face as he did a double take. "What the fu—"

"Now, don't start overreacting," Pooey said.

Kieron pushed Dora off him and jumped to his feet. He spun around to try to see his wings. It was a bit like watching a kitten chase its own tail. "What did you do to me?" he cried when he glanced at Dora.

"I didn't do that!" She protested, shaking her head.

"What are they? Am I deformed?" He stopped chasing them and stood over her with panic in his eyes.

Her eyes drank in his defined abs, tanned chest, beautiful face and the powerful peppered wings flapping behind him. "If you are deformed, I think everyone should be deformed like that." She told him, appreciating the view. He looked like an Adonis. If it hadn't been for the panic in his eyes, she was pretty certain her legs would have turned to jelly by now.

"You think it suits me?" He unsurely glanced back at his wings.

She nodded lots. The guy was glowing, literally. There was something innocent about him, but there was a darker side to him too. He was a demon-angel. *How does that even happen?*

"Contestants will be judged." A hollow voice echoed from the judge's platform.

Dora had forgotten about the tests. "Oh shit!" She gasped, quickly standing to face the judges. "Who won? What are we going to do?"

Kieron stood beside her and put his arm around her waist. "I don't know, but we're sticking together."

Pooey jumped up onto her shoulder. "I go where you go," he said.

They all stared up at the judges, waiting for the final judgment.

"Kieron D. Lascher, you have failed and will be exiled to Earth."

"Nooooo!" Lady Lascher screamed. She tried to cast a spell, but the sentries dragged her away.

"Don't worry, Mom. I want to study abroad!" Kieron shouted after her.

Dora fought not to laugh, but a smirk appeared on her face as Lady Lasher was bound magically, unable to speak or cast spells.

Dora's eyes settled on Lord Lascher. He had regained consciousness, and was now glaring at her. She narrowed her eyes and glanced at the staff near her feet. On impulse, she picked it up and pointed it at Lord Lascher, feeling a wicked grin form on her face. "Fuck you, asshole!" she shouted.

The crowds all turned to see what she had cast. She heard Lord Lascher yelp as a giant, hairy Minotaur materialized in the stands and ran towards him. The Minotaur wore black leather straps around his body. Silver spikes were embedded in his nipples, which led to chains he held in his cloven hands. She could hear the beast grunting as he chased Kieron's father through the stands and out of view.

There was a shocked moment of silence in the crowds that was eventually shattered by a knowing shriek from Lord Lascher. Dora chuckled.

"Was that entirely necessary?" Kieron asked.

She nodded a lot, trying to control her laughter.

The hollow voice echoed through the arena again. "Demonic Dora, you have failed and will be exiled to Earth."

She nodded and gripped Kieron's hand. She realized it didn't matter where she was, it only mattered who she was with. For years, she had tried to summon a demon, so she could get away from her parent's crazy, devout life, but even in Hell, she had not been safe. She had just traded one brainwashing prison for another. It wasn't the place that offered her freedom, it was believing she was free and knowing she always had a choice. In some ways, it was being around people who wanted her to be free as much as she did.

She gazed at Kieron. He had saved her, over and over again. Together they had freed each other. She didn't care where she went as long as it was with him. He made her happy, and he was the only family she needed.

Both of them had awful parents and horrific childhoods, but it didn't mean they had to continue living that way. It didn't matter where they ended up. They would be free wherever it was.

She smiled at Kieron, and he smiled back. He looked just like any other human boy now. His wings had gone back into the mystical ether they had come from. She wondered what he was, but decided that it didn't matter. He looked human right now.

"Personious Caelius, for interfering with a death match, you will be exiled to Earth," the judge said.

"Who the fuck is Personious?" Dora asked.

Pooey reluctantly raised his hand. "I prefer to be known as Pooey from now on," he muttered.

"Personious." Kieron laughed.

"Shut it, big bird." Pooey retaliated.

"So, er, what happens now?" Dora quickly interrupted before they began bickering.

Kieron and Pooey both shrugged. Clearly, this was all new to them too.

Vicious gusts of wind whipped around the arena, blasting against all three of them. They clung together as a portal opened in front of them. The portal roared as it became a vortex, sucking them into it. *Oh fuck!* Dora tried to keep her grip on Kieron's hand, but the force of the pull was too strong.

"Kieron!" she cried when she lost her grip on him, and the portal ripped him away from her. She tried to follow him, but the cyclone pulled her in another direction, and she spun out of control into an abyss.

"I'll find you!" She heard him shout as he disappeared from her view.

Pooey was gone. He had been holding her hair, but now he was nowhere to be seen.

*I'll find you both, I promise.* She told herself as the cyclone flung her deeper into the abyss. She let out a scream as the forces controlling her pulled her into the eye of the hurricane, told

dropped her like a stone down the center of it. She fell for a long time in total darkness before she hit something soft like a pillow.

She groaned and arched her back. *That landing fucking hurt.* It was pitch black, but she smelled earth around her. She had landed on some kind of silky cushion. She ran her fingers over the wood surrounding her, trying to work out where she had landed.

She frowned. It took a moment for her to realize where she was. *Oh, you have gotta be fucking kidding me. I'm in a bloody coffin!*

THE END

# READ THE NEXT BOOK

A MUST-READ NOVEL IN THE DEMON DIARIES

Deceased

DORA

DORA CARRIDINE
BEWITCHED
IN DEATH

CLAIRE CHILTON

## After being expelled from Hell, she woke up in her own coffin...

When Dora Carridine wakes up in her coffin, the first thing she plans to do is find out what happened to her friends since they were also exiled from Hell. But Dora didn't come back entirely human, and everyone keeps trying to kill her.

If she manages to avoid being bitten by an over-amorous, Victorian vampire, being captured by the Vatican and being roasted alive by her neighbors, then hopefully she can find Kieron and find out what she really is.

But first, she has to put an end to an ancient war amongst the paranormal beings on Earth. How hard can that be, right?

# OUT NOW

WWW.CLAIRE-CHILTON.COM

# CONTINUE READING WITH

# Divine DORA

## BEWITCHED IN HEAVEN

## CLAIRE CHILTON

# Heaven just turned out to be worse than Hell!

After being killed, Dora Carridine was shipped off to Heaven, but she's not ready to give up her life just yet, especially not when it means spending eternity in Angel boot camp.

She does everything in her power to try to get home, but nothing works. Even if she manages to escape Camp Angel and survive the sadistic drill sergeant, she still doesn't know how to get her body back.

Powerless and alone, she decides that there is only one thing she can do. Dora has to find God, and hope he's not a sanctimonious dick.

# CAN'T WAIT FOR CLAIRE CHILTON'S NEXT STORY?

Let her know by leaving stars and telling her what you liked about

# DEMONIC DORA

in a review!

-----------------------------------------

## FREE BOOKS

Enjoy Claire Chilton's free books. Try out her other series for free or read more of this series on any device with **Free Reads**.

**claire-chilton.com/free-books**

-----------------------------------------

## WANT TO TALK TO OTHER FANS?

Visit *claire-chilton.com* and join the discussion.

# AUTHOR

After completing her honors degree in English Literature, Claire Chilton was interviewed to work for MI5. Fortunately, for the sake of the United Kingdom, she did not get the job. Now a web designer and graphic designer with a passion for great stories, she writes about the adventures she'd like to have.

A prolific writer with wide-ranging interests, Claire specializes in romantic and speculative fiction, which includes genres such as mystery, science fiction, fantasy, horror, comedy and romance. Her mystery romance novel, *Hustle*, won Harlequin's *So You Think You Can Write* contest in 2013, and her previous books in *The Demon Diaries* won the *Most Read* award on Wattpad.

After exploring the world in her misspent youth, traveling across Europe, Africa, and the Caribbean, she now lives in an ancient Roman city in Yorkshire with her Californian husband and a fluffy kitten called Shadow, who is convinced she is a bigger cat than she is.

You can find Claire online at **claire-chilton.com**.